ALSO BY AMANDA HAMM

WEATHERING EVAN

THE 4ᵀᴴ FLOOR LOUNGE

MEET CUTE: 5 ROMANTIC SHORT STORIES

THE STORIES FROM HARTFORD SERIES
ANDREW'S KEY
JEALOUSY & YAMS
COLLECTING ZEBRAS
THE CHRISTMAS PROJECT
HEARTS ON THE WINDOW (EBOOK NOVELLA)

THE COFFEE AND DONUTS SERIES
SAID AND UNSAID
SOFIE WAITS
A PERFECTLY GOOD MAN
NOT COMPLICATED

THEY SEE A FAMILY
THE STUDY GROUP (EBOOK NOVELLA)

Everything Old

Amanda Hamm

ISBN: 978-1-943598-09-0

Everything Old is a work of fiction. All names, characters, places, events, etc. are products of the author's imagination or are used fictitiously.

1

Ruth was holding two stacked cheeseburgers when she slipped into the little knickknack shop. She hadn't been inside it since she was a child, and she felt like a child now because she was hiding from Mrs. Donnelly like one.

Nostalgia swept over Ruth at the sight of countless fragile objects on equally fragile glass shelves. The smell was even more potent at turning back time. It was a smell Ruth couldn't really describe except to say that it was what Granny's Shelf smelled like. That was the name of the little shop. Ruth had been in the shop only a few times with her mom – for purposes she could no longer remember – while the old woman who owned Granny's Shelf stared at her and made her feel as though she might break something if she breathed too strongly.

The shop was always eerily quiet, then and now. The old woman, who didn't appear to have changed either, stepped from around a corner without making a sound. She wrinkled her nose at the wrapped cheeseburgers in Ruth's hands as though they might smell of shattering glass.

Ruth forced a smile. "Hi... uh..."

"Can I help you?" The woman's voice was friendly, though her eyes were still flitting to the cheeseburgers with suspicion.

"No, I..." I just came in here to avoid someone. That was not a sentence Ruth intended to finish out loud. "This, uh..." She quickly scanned the nearest shelf for something she could describe as interesting. "This turtle is interesting. Do you mind if I just take a closer look?"

"Go ahead, dear."

Ruth took a step towards the shelf. She couldn't touch anything with her hands full, didn't want to touch anything with the owner watching so closely. She let her eyes skim over the turtle to a little white tag resting next to it on the shelf. Forty-five dollars? For a knickknack? Ruth could still honestly describe that as interesting. She glanced back, expecting impatience or irritation.

The eyes were still watching her closely. The thin lips were twitching, trying to hold back a smile. It seemed the woman knew that Ruth's entrance was merely a ruse of some sort, and she enjoyed watching her pretend otherwise.

Ruth was still not going to admit anything. "Uh, well... thank you," she said before she turned to the door. Mrs. Donnelly had surely rounded the corner by now. She had to stack the lunches to come inside but simply turned to push her back against the door to exit. She intended to wish the woman a nice afternoon as she left.

There was no one there. The old woman had evidently returned to somewhere deeper in the shop as quietly as she'd come out.

Ruth shrugged and stepped carefully onto the sidewalk. It was deserted in both directions. She exhaled slowly and walked the rest of the block to Mr. Sweet's office.

Ron Sweet was an insurance agent and Ruth's boss. The extra cheeseburger was not for him though. It was for Ella. Ella was two years older than Ruth and had worked there two years longer. She'd apparently spent much of those two years convincing Mr. Sweet – who also happened to be her father – that she could not fill the enormous shoes of his recently retired assistant by herself.

The first month after Ruth was hired had been rather awkward. She'd spent a lot of time feeling unhelpful while father and daughter rushed around trying to figure out the best way to split their workload with a third person. It had been a year now. Ruth felt like part of the team if not part of the family. She stacked the burgers once again to open the office door.

Ella was waiting just inside. She promptly snatched her lunch out of Ruth's hand. The paper crinkled loudly as she peeled it back. She closed her eyes as she took a bite.

"Sorry it took so long," Ruth said.

Ella's dark eyes opened and looked thoughtful. "Did it?"

"Maybe not." Ruth shrugged and began to open her own wrapper. Ducking into Granny's Shelf had only taken a minute. It probably wasn't long enough for anyone else to notice the delay. Ruth wanted to talk about it anyway. "I sort of took a detour to hide from Mrs. Donnelly."

"Mrs. Donnelly?" Ella flopped into her desk chair as she said the name.

Ruth sat at her own desk facing Ella's. An open door at the back of the room led to Mr. Sweet's private office. He could hear them and would come and lean against the doorframe if the topic drew his attention. It hadn't yet.

"Why were you hiding from Mrs. Donnelly?" Ella asked.

"You know very well why I was hiding from Mrs. Donnelly. It's August. Faith formation classes start in a few weeks, and I'm afraid she's going to ask me to volunteer."

"You want to get out of it this year?" Ella looked surprised. "I thought you liked teaching with your mom."

"I like that just fine." Ruth let that statement rest while she enjoyed a bite of her lunch. Mustard was the strongest flavor. Then cheese and juicy meat. It was a good burger. But she put it down to finish the conversation she'd started.

"Mom hinted some last year that after being her assistant I'd be ready to teach a class myself. It's – for obvious reasons – a lot harder to get volunteers to be main teachers than assistants so I just know someone is going to ask me to step up. I want it to be my mom because it'll be easier to say no to her than to Mrs. Donnelly."

Ella worked to swallow quickly because she was eager to talk. "You can say no to Mrs. Donnelly. I'll help you practice." She pushed her glasses down her nose. Mrs. Donnelly was always looking over the tops of her glasses. "Would you like to teach a faith formation class this year?"

"No," Ruth said.

"First graders are real cute. Would you be willing to teach first graders?"

Ruth's mouth was full. She just shook her head.

"Oh, I know." Ella's eyes twinkled over her red frames. "I could sign you up for one of the middle school classes. How about that?"

Ruth narrowed her eyes at her friend and shook her head a lot faster.

Movement in the doorway made both women look up as Mr. Sweet took his typical stance, arms folded and ankles crossed as he leaned against the doorway. He was a skinny man and considerably shorter than Ruth's dad and brothers. He'd lost half his hair when he was younger but the ring that was left was still fairly dark. His glasses had thin wire rims, and he didn't push them down to focus on Ruth. "Being a lead catechist would be that much more work?" he asked.

"It would," Ruth said. "When I work with my mom, I mostly

pass out papers and... Well, I only have to commit to being there for one hour a week. I don't have to commit to all the time it'd take me to prepare a lesson."

"I see." Ella put her glasses back into place. "You want to feel good about volunteering at the church without having to do a lot of actual work."

"Uh, yes. She's definitely afraid of work." Mr. Sweet nodded along with Ella, both of them clearly teasing.

Ruth knew they were teasing, knew she'd proven her work ethic in her time at the office. But something – it may have been her pride and it may have been guilt – made her defend herself nonetheless. "I am *not* afraid of work." She paused long enough to allow Mr. Sweet and his daughter to raise skeptical eyebrows to continue their teasing. Ruth did enjoy it despite her defensiveness. "What I'm afraid of is doing a lot of extra work and still being no good at it. I'm not a teacher."

"All kidding aside," Mr. Sweet said, looking more serious, "they do need assistant teachers. That is a valuable service. I'd have to suggest that your best defense in this case is a good offense."

"You mean I should volunteer to be my mom's assistant before she asks me to take a class myself?"

The phone rang as Ruth asked the question. Ella reluctantly took herself from the conversation to answer it.

Mr. Sweet nodded. "If you don't mind doing that again. Of course, you might still get asked to do the harder job, but it'll be easier to say no and to accept that no if it's because you're already helping in a different way."

The advice made a lot of sense. Ruth didn't have time to question it anyway before Ella used the intercom on her phone to make her voice come through her dad's office. "Mr. Sweet, Mrs.

Sweet is on line one for you."

Mr. Sweet smiled as he pushed himself from the door frame. He closed his door as he went into his office to take the call. His wife could have called his cell, but she liked to say hello to Ella at the same time.

"This was good," Ella said. She crumpled up the wrapper for the burger she'd finished. "I'm already thinking pizza for next week."

Ruth nodded. Though she was only halfway done with her own burger, pizza did sound good for their treat day. She and Ella brought lunches from home Monday through Thursday. They tried to include healthy food and reusable containers and everything else that made them feel like responsible young adults. Friday, however, was treat day. The people at Burger Brothers knew that. Ruth and/or Ella made an appearance there almost every other Friday.

"So... what do you think are the chances that St. Jude will get a young adult group going this year?"

Ruth smiled at Ella's hopeful expression. She shook her head though. "Not good. You know they've been trying to get one off the ground for like ten years now. It hasn't happened yet."

"It almost did though, right? Isaac was in it?"

"He went twice," Ruth clarified. Isaac was one of her older brothers. "He said there was hardly anyone there. Then he had to miss a few weeks for work or something and when he tried to go back the group didn't exist anymore."

"We need a leader who doesn't give up so easily." Ella pounded emphatically on her desk.

"Are you volunteering?"

She looked at the fist still on her desk, then guiltily folded her hands in her lap as she shook her head even more ardently than she'd pounded.

"That probably has something to do with why the group hasn't gotten off the ground."

Ella sighed. "True. I do hope that if something gets started, they don't do it the same night as the faith formation classes. You would need to come with me."

Ruth thought about that. "I don't think they'd do it the same night," she said. "That would eliminate some young adults from the pool of volunteer teachers."

"Ahh. Good point." Ella looked relieved that the group that wasn't going to happen was unlikely to have a scheduling conflict. Then a slow, sly smile bloomed. "And *if* we had a young adults group, do you think your brother would come?"

"I'm sure Isaac would be willing to try again." Ruth gave her a smug smile. They both knew that wasn't the brother Ella meant. "And he would bring Jessica."

Ella said nothing. She bunched up her mouth in what was intended as an angry face, but there was too much amusement in her eyes to pull it off.

The expression made Ruth laugh.

"You know I meant Joseph," Ella said. She stopped fighting her own smile.

"If you're interested in Joseph, you need to come with me when I visit my parents on Sundays."

"We tried that once. Remember?"

"I know, once. His schedule is kind of unpredictable." Ruth's older brother was a truck driver. He didn't do long hauls. Most of his trips were done in a day, but he had to start ridiculously early in the morning, times most people would consider the middle of the night, which made his sleep schedule unpredictable as well. His schedule changed week to week. On Sunday afternoons, when the rest of the family gathered, there was usually speculation on whether Joseph was working, sleeping, or on his way. "But he's there a lot. If you keep coming, you'll see him."

"That's a nice offer. If I start spending all my Sundays at your parents' house though, it won't be long before my parents start asking what I'm doing over there. Especially my mom."

"You'd be spending time with your best friend." Ruth smiled as she gave herself a slightly juvenile but still accurate title. "How is that suspicious?"

"I'm not sure suspicious is the right word but..." Ella paused to let out a groan. "You know how impatient my mom is about wanting grandchildren. I'm twenty-five and very single. She already knows you have three brothers. If I start spending time with your family, she'll be grilling me about who's there when I am and... I told you what she said last time, right?"

"About my cousins?" Ruth asked with a laugh.

"Yes." Ella was not laughing.

Ruth felt for her friend even though she was amused. When Ella last spent a Sunday afternoon with Ruth's family, her mom had been full of questions. She asked enough to learn that of Ruth's brothers one was married, one was engaged, and one wasn't there. Her next question had been, "Does Ruth have any cousins?" The answer was five. But they were all girls.

"Well," Ruth said, "if you don't want to come over every week, I could start texting Joseph every Sunday to see if he's coming and then let you know."

Ella chuckled nervously. She looked at Ruth as though she wasn't sure if she was kidding or not. "Do not do that," she said.

"Why not?" Ruth really wasn't sure if she was kidding either.

"Because if I start showing up only when Joseph is there, he will figure it out faster than my mom."

"Come on, you said yourself you're not twelve anymore."

Ruth crumpled the wrapper for the cheeseburger she'd finally finished. "Would it be sooo bad if a guy knew you were interested?"

"I guess not," Ella said even as her cheeks began to flame. "If I really was interested. But I don't know Joseph all that well. I'm just hoping he's as nice as you are. Because he's so cute."

Ruth made a gagging noise and then tried to toss her wrapper into the trash can. It bounced off the wall behind the trash and hit the floor near Ella's chair.

"Now who's twelve?" Ella picked up the wrapper and tossed it back for Ruth to try again. "Surely you can objectively admit that your brother is a nice-looking man."

Ruth concentrated on the trash can long enough to make her second shot. "No, I cannot," she said. "There are too many icky memories. Joseph and Isaac were six years ahead of me in school so I didn't have to put up with girls noticing them too much. But you know Adam was only two years ahead of me." He had been in Ella's class. "Plus he got a lot of attention from being a basketball star. Girls were always telling me how cute he was like I was lucky to have him in my house. Ew. A few times I even had girls try to buddy up to me to get close to him and this one time..." Ruth cringed as she called up the memory. "I overheard these two girls at a game talking about how he looked on the court. I had to change seats and I mean call me a prude, but I don't want to hear talk like that about anyone and this was my brother. I wanted to burn my ears out."

"Okay, that sounds bad." Ella waved her hand as though shooing the memory from the room. "But don't you think you're being a bit dramatic in general? It's not a big deal that you have three brothers who happen to be nice to look at. After all, *you* have benefited from those same genes."

"Thank you." Ruth acknowledged the compliment with a nod. "Let's not talk about this anymore though. How would you like it if I said your dad still looked pretty good for a sixty-one-year-old?"

Ella grimaced and held her stomach as though she was going to be sick. "Why did you have to go there?"

"What's the problem?" Ruth asked with false innocence. "Can't you admit that's objectively true?"

The inner door opened and Mr. Sweet stuck his head out. His eyes bounced warily from Ella to Ruth. "What are you girls doing out here?"

"Nothing, Dad." Ella shot Ruth a look that threatened serious retribution if she didn't stay silent.

Ruth knew her eyes were communicating the same threat. The lid had been slammed shut on the topic.

2

Gabriel Chadwick flipped the tie around his neck and tied it with a practiced hand. His grandfather had given him the blue paisley one, and it was probably his favorite. His mom always said it highlighted the blue in his eyes, which was the reason it was probably his favorite and not definitely his favorite. He just liked the pattern and could do without the comments.

Not a lot of guys wore ties to church anymore, particularly guys Gabriel's age. Gabriel didn't mind being different though. He did not consider old-fashioned an insult.

He stuffed his phone in one pocket and his wallet in another. Then he picked up his keys and walked to the front door. Sun beat down on his head as he locked it behind himself. It would be a hot walk to church, but at least it would be a short one.

Gabriel had lived in his apartment only a few months. It was a brick building with four units. It sat on a quiet corner of the quiet town. St. Jude's was exactly one block away. The church had a small parking lot so a lot of people parked on the street. If he drove to church, he'd have to leave pretty early to get a spot any closer than in front of his building where he started.

The church was over a hundred years old but had been remodeled a few times. Gabriel loved the heavy wooden doors, which he knew had not been replaced. He grabbed the iron handle and stood back to hold the door for an older couple arriving at the same time. They smiled and thanked him politely. He entered behind them and walked very slowly up the steps to avoid crowding them. The man leaned intensely on the railing while his wife leaned intensely on him.

Gabriel entered the sanctuary and his eyes instinctively sought out his parents near the front in their usual seat. His dad's family had lived in Andauk, OH long enough and attended St. Jude's long enough that the pew had at one time quite literally had their name on it. His dad liked to sit there to feel connected to the past, but he didn't feel any ownership of the pew. If someone else got there first, he certainly wouldn't hold any grudge.

Gabriel didn't always sit with his parents. Sometimes he preferred to sit alone. But his mom happened to turn around as he came in. She waved happily. This was going to be a Sunday that he sat with his parents. He walked up the aisle and took the seat next to her.

They sat peacefully in familiar silence for a few minutes before Gabriel's older brother appeared in the aisle. Gabriel and his parents scooched a little closer to make room for Eric.

Their mom smiled as he sat down and whispered, "The whole family is here."

Gabriel smiled at her, then turned to his brother so they could share an eye roll at her excitement. Eric had arrived just in time for the Mass to start. He and Gabriel grabbed hymnals to find the gathering song while their parents shared a book already opened to the right page.

It wasn't his favorite song, but it was recognizable enough for Gabriel to sing along with little thought. He listened to the readings, and he went up for communion. He returned to the pew and knelt between his mom and his brother. Then he closed his eyes and tried to concentrate on not watching the rest of the congregation file past. He was not going to look for her. It was a habit he really needed to break because the reminders were not doing him any favors. His eyes opened on their own. He saw a few familiar faces. Actually, he saw a lot of familiar faces. Andauk was a small town, and he'd been part of this church his whole life. He could trace at least loose connections to most of the people walking past.

And there in the midst of them was Ruth Ziebert. Goodness, she was pretty. Her straight red hair was halfway down her back. It was so much longer than it'd been in high school and seemed to emphasize how long it'd been since they'd spoken. The one that got away.

Gabriel sighed and rested his forehead on his folded hands. He hated that saying. It was trite and annoying and in this case not even true. She would have had to have been his in the first place to have gotten away from him. No matter how hard he tried, he could not stop the words from popping into his head every time he saw her. They were more annoying than usual with Eric sitting next to him. They might've been true for Eric.

Thoughts of Ruth were successfully pushed aside for the rest of the Mass. His mom leaned over him at the conclusion to ask Eric something. He let them talk over him for a minute as the aisles cleared. Then his dad stood and motioned the family to follow him as there seemed to be more room on his side.

The next thing Gabriel knew, his mom was pushing on his chest and tugging her husband's arm to get them both to turn around. "Mrs. Donnelly's over there," she said. "I can't sign up for anything else right now."

Gabriel turned around with a knowing sigh. Mrs. Donnelly was always recruiting volunteers for something or other going on at the church and his mother was always saying yes to more than she could handle. She'd recently resolved not to over-commit herself. She planned to say no to anything new but apparently only if she could avoid being asked in the first place.

The crowd made its way to the exits funneling around various groups who had stopped to chat. Somehow, despite his mom's efforts, the Chadwick family ended up bumping into Mrs. Donnelly just outside the door. Gabriel bit back a smile as she recognized them. He sensed his mom stiffen as the woman locked eyes on them.

"Gabriel Chadwick," she said, "just the person I was looking for."

Gabriel had already turned to his mom before he realized she wasn't the one being addressed. He looked back at Mrs. Donnelly in surprise.

She was fiftyish. She'd been a few years ahead of his mom in school, but he couldn't remember exactly how many and didn't care. He did care that she had pushed her glasses down to make eye contact over the tops of the frames, something she seemed to do whenever she spoke to someone one-on-one.

"Yes?" he said.

"I suppose you know we're trying to start up a young adult group this year?"

He nodded at her, unable to look away from the piercing gaze.

"Of course we're going to need some young adults to lead the group," she continued. "We're hoping to get two volunteers so that the burden doesn't rest entirely on one set of shoulders."

Gabriel kept nodding. He understood exactly where the conversation was heading, and it would not be a problem. He would simply take the opportunity to show his mom how this saying no thing was done.

"I was talking to the pastor about it and your name came to mind immediately. I thought that Gabriel Chadwick, he's a nice responsible young man. He would do a great job leading our other young people." Mrs. Donnelly glanced away to include his parents in the positive appraisal.

Gabriel tipped his head in deference to the compliment. He was responsible. He'd been an altar server for eight years, which was only part of the reason he could say no to something else without feeling guilty. Even if he wasn't currently serving the church in any way.

Mrs. Donnelly leaned in for the kill. "I knew all we needed was to get you a solid partner to get this ministry off the ground. So I spoke to Ruth Ziebert's mom just before Mass and she's pretty sure we can get Ruth on board. What do you say? Can we count on you?"

What did he say? He was going to say no. Of course he was going to say no. How could he possibly volunteer to work with Ruth when she'd probably end up breaking his heart? Again. But Mrs. Donnelly didn't know what she was asking. He needed to find a polite, calm way out of it. Maybe, if he was lucky, there would be a practical reason he couldn't do it. "When would this group meet?" he asked.

"Friday evenings. We already have the teachers' lounge in the school reserved for 7 to 8:30, though we could shift the time a bit earlier or later if you like." The eyes over the glasses continued their hopeful questioning.

"No, 7 o'clock would be a good time," Gabriel said, forgetting to add that it would be a good time *if* he was going to lead it. He might like to attend some of the meetings if he was honest with himself. He just wasn't going to be the one leading them. Not if it meant working with Ruth. He couldn't do that.

"Very good." Mrs. Donnelly smiled, almost as though the matter was settled.

"And what would we talk about?" Gabriel was legitimately curious, though he felt bad that his questions were leading Mrs. Donnelly into believing he might agree. He should tell her he wasn't interested in leading before asking anything else.

"Saints. It'll be so easy because there are so many saints you'll never run out. All you and Ruth will have to do is pick a saint each week and come up with a few questions to spark the discussion. Then you're off to the races."

Gabriel found himself nodding along with what she was saying despite the big fat no he was about to unleash. She would no longer describe him as a nice young man after he got her hopes up and then stomped on them.

"I've already written up the copy for next week's bulletin," she said, "so you could start the following week. I just have to fill in the leaders' names."

"Okay," Gabriel said. It was time to tell her there was no way he could be talked into leading the group. "I'll do it."

"Wonderful!" She pushed her glasses back over her eyes to include the rest of his family in her satisfaction. "Send me an email with your phone number and as soon as I hear from Ruth, I'll send you each other's contact info. Let me know if you need anything else as you get started. I'm happy to help." She waved to all of them before she rushed off to talk to some other fully-suspecting victim.

"Well, that was interesting."

"Yeah, I guess she wasn't after you this time, Mom." Gabriel turned as he spoke and realized Eric was no longer standing with them. He must have slipped away thinking he'd be the second choice after Gabriel said no. He did see a couple of his parents' friends moving their way. Time to make his own exit. "I'll see you two later," he said with a wave.

"Bye, Gabriel."

The sun was hotter now that it was closer to noon. Gabriel pulled his tie loose as he walked home. It wasn't the heat that was making him feel strangled though. It was the fact that he'd just proven himself a glutton for punishment. No matter how hard he tried to convince himself otherwise, he'd known he was going to help with the stupid new group the moment Ruth's name entered the conversation. He was so weak. He would have to give his mother a lesson in saying no some other time.

3

Ruth went home after church to change her clothes before she went to her parents' house. She swapped her sundress for shorts and a t-shirt, which wasn't that much more comfortable than the dress. But she was very happy to kick off the strappy sandals for soft tennis shoes. Her feet needed to be comfortable if anyone challenged her to some basketball after lunch.

The trip to her parents' house wasn't much of a trip. She pretty much lived in their backyard. What was once a detached garage had been converted to a detached mother-in-law suite shortly before they bought the property. The building had a decent-sized bedroom with a tiny kitchen and tiny bathroom. Ruth liked to feel as though she had her own place because she was paying rent, but she could never forget that it was very much in her parents' backyard.

Joseph had lived there first. He moved in shortly after he finished high school and stayed for about six years. Isaac went to college and returned to his old bedroom on breaks. Ruth had thought the brother living on his own had seemed the more mature and grownup of the pair. Now that she was twenty-three and living on her parents' property, it didn't seem as grownup.

She could not, however, turn down what was significantly lower rent than she'd find elsewhere just to feel more independent.

As much as she enjoyed working with Ella and Mr. Sweet, the job didn't pay very well and she had student loans to pay back.

A narrow sidewalk led from Ruth's front door to her parents' back door. From there, she had a good view of the side street where they all parked. A car pulled in behind hers. She recognized the car and Isaac and his wife Jessica inside it. The two of them had met in college and got married the summer after they graduated. Just before their seventh anniversary, they announced that the first grandchild was on the way. Jessica got out of the car first. She was very thin and only five months pregnant so the baby made a cute little bump. She wore her blond hair to her shoulders with thick bangs and a slight wave.

As Isaac joined his wife, Ruth very unwillingly tried to objectively examine his appearance while she hated Ella for putting the idea in her head. He was over six feet tall, which Ella might have found appealing. He was a redhead like most of the family. He had the typical coloring that went with it, light freckled skin. His eyes were blue, regular blue. Ruth didn't spot any major flaws. No big nose, sticky-out ears, or weird asymmetry. That was as far as she could go on determining attractiveness.

Isaac waved. "Hey, Baby Ruth."

Ruth ignored him and smiled at Jessica. They'd all called her Baby Ruth when she was little. Fortunately, most of the family had outgrown the nickname about the same time she did. She let Isaac get away with Baby Ruth only because he didn't do it in public. This was not because of a kind impulse on his part. It was because he absolutely dreaded being called Ike, which gave Ruth the means to retaliate if he ever slipped.

"I smell cinnamon," Jessica said. "Do you guys smell cinnamon?"

Isaac shook his head.

Ruth inhaled deeply through her nose. She hadn't noticed before but with a deliberate effort, she found the spice in the air. "Oh, I think I do." She looked at Jessica. "I wonder what Mom's making."

"Let's find out," Isaac said. He jumped up the steps to pull open the door for his wife. Then he hurried after her to let it slam in his sister's face.

Ruth rolled her eyes at the screen door before she let herself in.

Their mother was standing in the kitchen over a glass bowl beating the yellowy contents with a whisk. Isaac must have already asked her what she was making because she immediately said, "Puffy pancakes with cinnamon apples. I chopped the apples and set them to simmer before church so all I need to do is get this in the oven, then it will be twenty minutes until lunch."

"Do you need any help, Mom?" Jessica asked.

"Thanks, dear. I've got things under control though. You all have a seat, and I'll be with you soon." She let go of the whisk and motioned them towards the living room.

Joseph was already in there chatting with his dad. Greetings flew around the room as the newcomers found places to sit.

"Is Adam coming?" Ruth asked the room at large.

Her dad shook his head.

Joseph restarted the story he'd been telling. His truck had broken down a few days earlier. When he was told it'd be at least two hours before a tow arrived, he lay down in the grass for a nap. He'd woken up to find a police officer standing over him. Someone had apparently thought he'd been thrown from the truck and called 911.

Ruth laughed at his impression of the officer telling him to try to look "less dead" the next time he decided to take a nap outside. Then, before she could stop herself, her mind went again to Ella saying Joseph was cute. He had, on occasion, been jokingly referred to as the black sheep of the family. He was the only one in the immediate family who didn't have red hair. His was dark brown or black, depending on who was asked. It was also curly, unlike anyone else's. He seemed happy to emphasize the differences though. While both of his brothers kept their hair buzzed close to the scalp, he let his get shaggy and hang nearly in his eyes, which were brown. He wasn't quite as tall as Isaac or Adam, and Ruth was glad her mom entered the room before she spent any more time looking at her brother.

"Lunch smells really good, honey," her dad said as her mom sat on the couch between him and Ruth.

Joanna Ziebert accepted the praise with a smile. "I talked to Mrs. Donnelly this morning." She glanced around the room as she spoke. Her eyes seemed to linger on Ruth, but Ruth might have imagined that. "Looks like I'll be teaching first grade faith formation again this year.

Several people nodded. This was not surprising at all. Ruth's mom was a teacher during the day as well and had been most of her adult life, though she took some time off after each of her children were born.

Ruth saw the opportunity to get ahead of being asked to teach a class. "Did you sign me up to be your assistant again?" she asked. "I'd be okay with that."

Her mom opened her mouth but didn't say anything.

The hesitation was worrisome. "You need an assistant, right?" Ruth prompted. Of course her mom needed an assistant, but Mrs. Donnelly had gotten to her first. The woman had likely convinced her to take a new assistant to leave Ruth free to volunteer as a lead teacher.

"Well... I would welcome your help." Her mom spoke slowly, carefully. "But I'm not sure you'd have time if... Mrs. Donnelly has something different in mind for you."

All right, if Ruth had to say no, she had to say no. At least she could say it to her mom. "Mom, I just don't think I'm cut out for teaching. I can't command a class like you do. I think it's better for everyone if I stay a helper."

Her mom smiled. It was an odd smile because it didn't seem to be in response to the compliment or the alternate volunteering that Ruth was doing. It looked guilty about something.

"No one says no to Mrs. Donnelly," Joseph teased. "You're gonna have to teach some kids, sis."

"It's only an hour a week," Jessica added. "You can do that." She sounded encouraging, but Jessica was also a trained elementary school teacher. It was easy for her to say.

"Mrs. Donnelly actually has all the teachers she needs," her mom said.

Joseph nodded. "Told you no one says no."

If that was true though, why did Ruth still feel as though her mom was trying to ask something more of her?

"Mrs. Donnelly said they're finally going to get the young adult group started this year and they need leaders for that."

"Oh." Ruth wasn't immediately sure how she felt about that. She was interested in joining a young adult group. She was much less interested in leading one. But someone had to do it.

"She said they'd get two leaders so you wouldn't have to do it alone."

Maybe Ruth could get Ella to lead with her.

"Mrs. Donnelly already has someone in mind for the other leader. She was sure she just needed to get confirmation."

Ella probably wouldn't want to lead anyway. Ruth would still get her to come though. The group needed members.

"You could take turns so you only have to lead every other week or work together. Whatever the two of you decide is easier."

"Wait," Ruth said. The coleader could definitely turn this into something fun or something disastrous. "Who does Mrs. Donnelly have in mind to be the other leader?"

"She didn't say."

"Oh." That was a problem. What if Ruth agreed to do this and then found out she had to work with someone she could hardly stand to be around?

"I, uh..." Joanna Ziebert started slowly, looking guilty again. "I kind of told Mrs. Donnelly that I thought I could talk you into it."

Ruth sighed while her brothers snickered.

"I also told her I could recruit a few members," she added.

Both boys and Jessica shrugged and nodded. Joining was not the same as being asked to be in charge.

"What do you say, Ruth?" Her mom looked at her expectantly.

Ruth supposed that she could always quit if it turned out to be awful. And she might not even have to quit. This had been tried before and failed before. She might only be committing herself to two or three weeks of leading a group. "All right," she said. "You can tell Mrs. Donnelly you talked me into it."

"Wonderful! It'll start a week from Friday. I'll let her know you're in and she should send you contact info for your coleader in the next few days. Then you can get started planning."

4

Ruth told Ella about her new responsibility first thing Monday morning. Ella was excited. The two of them spent the next few days speculating on who the coleader could be. They tried to think of anyone close to their age who went to their church. A lot of the people they'd had faith formation classes with no longer showed up on Sundays, at least that they could remember seeing. There were still quite a few names though.

Ella suggested Eric Chadwick, who had been in her class. He was a nice guy. He'd been Adam's friend for a long time. Ruth thought she could work with him, though she couldn't think of any reason he would have come to Mrs. Donnelly's mind as a leader candidate. Not that Ruth knew why she'd been selected either.

Then of course Ella suggested Eric's brother Gabriel, which made Ruth hold her breath while she considered that possibility. What were the odds Mrs. Donnelly would pick someone with whom Ruth had history, very awkward history? She didn't know why the woman would think of Gabe any more than Eric or any of the other names they'd come up with. It was a good thing St. Jude's didn't depend on Ruth to come up with volunteers. She put Gabe Chadwick out of her head. It was too uncomfortable to think about him.

Finally, on Wednesday evening, Ruth got the email she'd been waiting for. Mrs. Donnelly thanked her for agreeing to lead the new ministry. She told her they'd be tasked with discussing saints and recommended a few books she could find at the library for biographies and possible discussion questions. And then she innocently dropped the bomb of the other leader's name. Gabriel Chadwick. There was a familiar email under his name and a phone number that was still the first contact in Ruth's phone.

She went to work the next morning desperate to talk to Ella about the new development and just as desperate to *not* talk to Mr. Sweet about it. Ella didn't appreciate the need to wait for good timing. She asked if Ruth had heard from Mrs. Donnelly during the first quiet moment at the start of the day.

"Yes," Ruth said simply. "I got an email last night."

"And?" Ella raised her eyebrows expectantly. She was wearing contacts. Ruth couldn't see them of course but knew they were there because Ella was not wearing one of her many pairs of glasses.

"Gabe Chadwick." Ruth thought she said the name very plainly. She must have given something away though.

Ella smiled almost smugly. She stared searchingly at Ruth for what felt like several minutes. At last she said, "All right. If he's going to be your coleader, you're finally going to have to tell me what the deal is."

"What deal?"

Ella snorted. "What deal indeed? I thought you two dated in high school, but you told me you were only ever friends. That's the only thing you've told me. But his name has come up a few times and you get weird."

"Weird how?"

"You just did it. It was like a mental flinch when you said his name. I'm sensing a story."

Ruth moved her eyes to the open door of Mr. Sweet's office and back to Ella.

She understood. Her eyes got a little wider. "That good, huh?" She glanced out the window. "Okay. We'll take our lunch outside today, and you can tell me then."

Lunchtime arrived faster than a good song is cranked up. It seemed to Ruth that they'd just put off the conversation when Ella pulled two bags out of the mini fridge and set one on Ruth's desk. She walked to the door of her father's office while Ruth finished the form she was filling out. "Dad, we're going to eat outside today. Is that okay?"

"Sure." His voice carried out to Ruth. "You girls have a nice break."

Ella took her lunch to the front door and waited for Ruth to follow.

There were several wooden benches along Main Street. The office was on the main street of town, and it was actually called Main Street. Ruth wasn't thinking about the street name as she sat on the bench though. Ella was clearly not thinking about it either. She hadn't even opened her lunch when she said, "Let's start at the beginning."

Ruth stalled. She opened her sandwich box and took a bite of peanut butter and jelly. It was on whole wheat bread sprinkled with other seeds and grains, something she would not have eaten as a kid. She wasn't stalling because she didn't want to talk about it but because she really wasn't sure what the beginning of the story was.

"Tell me how you and Gabriel became friends," Ella said. "Was that in high school?"

"No. We were friends almost before I can remember." Saying that out loud, with past tense, gave Ruth a pang of how much she missed her old friend. In the middle of all her fears of coming awkwardness was hope that they could get something back.

Ella still hadn't started her lunch. "Did you live near each other? Stop making me guess the story."

"All right." Ruth took one more bite and then put her sandwich down. "We had brothers in the same grade. Eric and Adam were friends first. Right from kindergarten, I think. Our moms arranged some playdates for them and they became friends, our moms. So sometimes they got the whole families together and sometimes Gabe and I had to tag along because we were little. We were just thrown together so much that we became good friends, too."

Ella nodded. She started picking off pieces of her sandwich and eating it like popcorn in a movie theater.

"By the time we got to high school, a lot of people thought we were a couple. I don't think Gabe put much effort into correcting the rumor just because he's always been good at not caring what other people think. I didn't go around telling people we were only friends because... Well, two reasons."

"And one of them was because you were secretly in love with him?" Ella asked.

Ruth frowned at her. "I thought you didn't want to guess the story."

"Sorry. Was that one of the reasons though?"

"Not exactly."

Ella prompted her to continue with a nod.

"The first reason was kind of stupid. I wasn't allowed to date. My parents said I couldn't date until I was seventeen. No one was going to ask me out if they thought I already had a boyfriend. I thought that would save me the embarrassment of... I don't know. I thought it sounded babyish to say I wasn't allowed to date." Ruth paused in her story because Ella seemed to find something amusing. "What?"

"My parents had the same rule, although they said sixteen. I was seventeen the first time a guy asked me out and I told him I still wasn't allowed to date. I guess I was more scared of going on a date than of sounding like a baby."

"Huh." Ruth smiled. "Does that mean one of us was weird?"

Ella smiled back. "It was you," she said, then ducked away from a playful shove. "Okay, I only interrupted because you asked a question. What was the other reason?"

"I thought we'd eventually end up together." Ruth shrugged and tried to explain why this wasn't also a stupid reason. "We got along so well and could talk about anything. We did sometimes talk about the future, only in general or hypothetical terms, but we wanted and believed the same things. I couldn't think of a better person to *someday* build a life with. I thought we'd end up married. Then, for college, you know I went to Bowling Green and he went to Toledo."

"Why did you go to different schools?" Ella asked. "And please don't tell me you drifted apart. That's too sad. I mean, I don't think it's more than a thirty minute drive between those schools."

"Depends who's driving," Ruth said. She picked up her sandwich.

Ella waited while she had a few more bites because they did need to get back to work before long. She didn't exactly wait patiently. Her feet were tapping on the sidewalk and her eyes kept saying it was time to get to the good part.

"Once we got to school," Ruth started, "something changed." She tried to find the right words. "In high school, we had a lot of classes together and town or school events and our parents getting together and we just kind of saw each other all the time without any fuss. It was a given that we were walking to his house after school or doing a project together or... Anyway, when we started college, we had to deliberately make plans to see each other and that – at least to me – started to kind of feel like we were dating. Plus, I was noticing more and more that he was... well, a guy."

"Aw." Ella kind of sighed but didn't really interrupt.

"I didn't know if it'd be better to talk first about the relationship or just wait until he kissed me because I seriously thought that was going to happen any day." Ruth stopped and put her teeth on her lower lip. They were getting to the terrible part. Mental flinch seemed like a good way to describe her thoughts.

Ella nudged her. "So what happened?"

"I, uh... well, I *think*... that I *accidentally*... went out with his brother instead."

Confusion covered Ella's face for about five seconds before she burst out laughing. "I'm sorry," she said between gasps, trying to get a hold of herself. "I'm sorry. It's just the way you... you *think* you *accidentally* went out with Eric? How do you accidentally go out with someone? And how do you not know?"

"Are you finished laughing at me?"

"Yes." Ella wiped her hand over her face, which wasn't necessary. She'd sobered up pretty quickly after the initial shock. "Please, tell me."

"Okay. So I told you that we became friends through Adam and Eric. They were still close this whole time, too. My first year of school was Adam's third. And that's when he dropped out. It wasn't *that* big of a deal that he dropped out, it was the way he did it. He came home for Christmas break having already officially withdrawn. He didn't even take his first semester finals. But he didn't tell anyone until the day before we were supposed to go back, and then he refused to talk about it at all. My parents were worried. They thought something must have happened."

Ella was nodding along, but she looked impatient to find out what Adam had to do with the story.

"Hang on," Ruth said. "This is important. About a week after I got back to school, Eric called me. Actually, Gabe texted me first, and I didn't think anything of it until I started to go back and analyze the situation. It said, 'Eric wants to call you. I hope it's okay that I gave him your number.'"

Ella's expression looked something like a wince. It seemed she already picked up the potential significance.

"In hindsight," Ruth said, preparing to defend herself, "I can see how that sounds like he might have been trying to gauge whether or not I was interested in Eric, but at the time... Well, I only had two thoughts. The first was that I was kind of surprised Eric didn't already have my number. I mean, with our families getting together a lot I thought it might have come up at some point, but then I didn't have his number either. Mostly, though, what I thought was that he wanted to talk about Adam. I thought he knew something about what was going on and wanted to maybe ask my opinion on whether or not to tell my parents or have me tell them."

"Oh." Ella mashed her lips together thoughtfully. "I can actually see how that would have made sense."

"Thank you," Ruth said. "I hadn't seen a lot of Eric since he started school, but we'd always been friendly. I didn't think of him as... like that."

"When did you figure out he was interested in you?"

"I... I'm not sure he was. I'm still not... He called me, asked if we could grab lunch. We met at the Taco Bell near campus, certainly not a romantic destination. It was a casual lunch. We just chatted and caught up a bit. I kept waiting for him to bring up Adam. At some point, I asked him if he knew if something had happened, and he shrugged it off like there wasn't anything specific to worry about. That's when I started to wonder why he suddenly wanted to talk to me if it wasn't about my brother. There was a slightly tense vibe for a bit where I think maybe we were both wondering if the other thought it was a date. I don't know. He didn't call me again, and it hasn't been weird when we've bumped into each other since."

"Back to you and Gabe," Ella said, "because I'm wondering how he took this... development."

"I thought we'd almost laugh about it. I'd say something like, 'I thought your brother wanted to talk to me about my brother, but he didn't. What do you think that was about?' Then he'd say, 'I don't know. I hope he didn't think it was a date.'"

Ella tipped her head to the side with a skeptical expression.

"Yeah, it's not funny. I didn't really think we'd laugh. But I thought it'd be easy enough to explain. I never got a chance. Gabe said he was too busy to get together that weekend, which I'm pretty sure was the first weekend we hadn't seen each other since we'd started school. I got one word responses to a few texts, also unusual, and then – this is so stupid – but I basically got mad at him for being mad at me and all of a sudden it'd been weeks since we had any contact. Then it was too hard. I didn't have the guts to apologize, and it got harder the more time went by. Now it's been almost four years."

"Wow. That's sad."

"I know." Ruth sighed. She closed her lunch, as she no longer had the appetite to finish it. "That's why I flinch. I regret so much about the way things fell apart."

"Maybe Mrs. Donnelly did you a favor. If you're forced to work together, it could end up being just like old times." Ella offered an encouraging smile.

Ruth forced a smile in return. She did want a second chance, but she wasn't sure she wanted it to be like old times. She saw Gabe around town occasionally and didn't have any trouble objectively observing that he was a very nice-looking young man. It would be difficult to be satisfied with their old friendship.

5

It wasn't as though Ruth had spent four years fretting over how things had worked out with Gabe. Or rather, how things had *not* worked out. Sure, there was a pang or two when she was reminded, but most of the time she'd done a pretty good job of moving on and not thinking about him at all.

Not thinking about Gabriel Chadwick became much harder to do after Ruth got that email from Mrs. Donnelly. Ruth needed to call him so they could get to work planning the meetings she didn't know how to plan. Every time she tried, four years of anxiety came out of the woodwork to press down on her. She could remember so clearly how she'd felt trying to call him in the past. There had been a need to talk to him and a fear of rejection and the irrational belief that putting it off one more day would give her the necessary courage to make the call. Until one more day had turned into so many days she was convinced he'd given up on the friendship.

In the present, those fears were mixed with feelings of foolishness and the delusion that Ruth wasn't actually putting off the phone call. She was simply waiting for a better time. There had been stuff going on, and she couldn't call him right now because her parents were expecting her for lunch.

Ruth stepped outside. Her sidewalk was dry, but remains of the previous night's thunderstorm still pooled in patches of the grass. The line of cars told her that Isaac and Adam had arrived. They dressed casually for church and didn't feel the need to change first so they usually arrived before Ruth even though they didn't live in their parents' backyard. There was also a white sedan on the road, one that Ruth knew belonged to Mr. and Mrs. Chadwick.

Her parents usually got together with the Chadwicks on other days of the week. Her mom had mentioned before church that it'd been too long since she'd seen them so she planned to invite them over for lunch. They'd apparently accepted.

Ruth began to walk slower. She thought that Gabe's parents were nice people, and she wouldn't have been concerned if Ella hadn't told her she flinched when someone said his name. Now Ruth was wondering if everyone could see her reaction. She sighed as she realized she had stopped walking altogether. She willed her feet to start moving and stop being childish. It wouldn't be that bad. If someone did mention Gabe, she would steer the conversation to the young adult group they were supposed to lead. Any anxiety on her face could easily and correctly be attributed to not knowing how to lead the group.

She could hear voices and laughter coming through the screen door before she pulled it open. She stepped into the kitchen and came face to face with Gabriel Chadwick.

"Hi," he said.

Ruth said, "Hi." She was otherwise frozen by the surprise. Andauk was a small town. It wasn't as though she hadn't seen him at all in years. Particularly the last year that they'd both been back from school, she'd bumped into him at church or the grocery store or somewhere else they could simply say hello and keep walking. They'd acknowledged each other the same as any other familiar face in town. But Ruth couldn't just keep walking after bumping into him in her parents' kitchen. She stood there with her mouth slightly open instead.

Gabe looked over his shoulder and called, "Ten minutes!"

Ruth jumped, partly at the volume of his voice but mostly she hadn't expected him to say anything. She had kind of thought they were going to stare awkwardly at each other until someone else came into the room.

He smiled apologetically, which caused tiny dimples to appear on his face and confirmed that Ruth had jumped as violently as she thought because he'd noticed. "Your mom sent me in here to see how much time was left on the oven timer," he explained. "Sorry if, uh... Did you see the ad in the bulletin for Friday?"

"No." Ruth shook her head. Why hadn't she checked? She wasn't in the habit of reading the bulletin, but she knew there'd be a notice about Friday. It would be a good idea to know what people might be expecting.

"I'll get it." Gabe slipped into the living room for only a few seconds before he returned with a paper showing a picture of St. Jude's on the front. He opened it to find the right page.

Ruth watched him as she told herself to relax. It was the first time she'd ever felt underdressed for visiting her own parents. Gabe was wearing navy slacks with a white dress shirt and recognizable tie. It had swirls in various shades of blue, and he'd had it since high school. She smiled to think he might like it more with every year older it got. She also smiled at the horn-rimmed glasses. Those were new and oddly flattering. The eyes behind them had the lids lowered to skim the bulletin, covering blue that hadn't changed. They popped open.

"I found it," he said. He turned the paper to face Ruth with his finger on the bottom of a page.

She stepped closer to read what it said.

St. Jude's will be starting a young adult ministry (20s and 30s, single or married) on Fridays from 7:00 to 8:30 PM in the teachers' lounge on the first floor of the school. Join Gabriel Chadwick and Ruth Ziebert to discuss the inspiration and example of the Saints.

****

He could feel Ruth's breath on his fingers as he held the bulletin out. He wanted her to take it so he could step back. There was a wall of tension in the room. With Ruth standing right in front of him, Gabriel sensed there was sweet familiarity on the other side of the wall. It was so far out of reach he didn't even know how to try.

Ruth finished studying the ad – it could not have taken her so long to simply read it – and moved to a more comfortable distance. She bit the side of her lip and said, "We're supposed to be inspirational?"

The doubtful tone made Gabriel slightly more at ease. She'd taken out a brick and that was a start. "The saints are inspirational," he said, "not us."

"But the saints won't be in the room. If they're going to be inspirational, it'll only be because we bring up the right things or ask the right questions."

"You might have a point. That's why we should probably start talking about what we want to talk about."

She squinted at him as though he didn't make any sense.

Gabriel could tell she knew what he meant and was only giving him a hard time. "At the meeting," he said anyway. "We should figure out what we want to discuss at the meeting. I got the books Mrs. Donnelly suggested from the library. I got two of them anyway, one was checked out."

"Do you have them here?"

He pointed over his shoulder because he'd left them in the living room. "I haven't read them, but I skimmed through one. It has discussion questions. I see no reason we can't use some of them if we like them."

Ruth nodded silently.

It would have been better if she said something. Gabriel wanted to know if she was pleased that he'd already picked up the books or annoyed that he'd started without her.

"After lunch," she said. "We'll talk about it after lunch." She moved past him to greet her family, which was after all why she was there. She was there to see her family so it shouldn't have felt as though she was leaving the room to avoid him. It still felt as though she was leaving the room to avoid him.

Gabriel followed slowly. He heard Adam say, "So who's Batman and who's Robin?" as he entered the living room.

When no one immediately answered, Gabriel looked around and realized the question was directed at him. "What?" he asked.

Adam pointed at Gabriel then at Ruth. "You and Ruth doing this thing at church. Which of you is really in charge and which of you is just the sidekick?"

"I... think we'll work together."

Ruth said, "Gabe can be Batman if he wants to."

She had a dismissive tone and only looked at Adam. Maybe she wasn't pleased or annoyed that he brought the books because she was indifferent to working with him. Or worse, maybe she wanted out of the whole thing now that she knew who her partner was.

Isaac was laughing.

"What's so funny?" Ruth asked him.

"I'm picturing Gabriel as Batman," he said. "He'd be driving around in a Batmobile that's like a souped-up Model T with a tape deck."

Laughter swelled around the room, which Gabriel enjoyed because he knew the teasing was in fun. "That would be sweet," he said. "I could find a place on the utility belt for my phone." He pulled it from his pocket and slid out the keypad for everyone to go ahead and mock.

Kayla, Adam's fiancée, said, "Oh my goodness." She said it the same way a person might react to the sight of a horrific car accident. Then she used her phone, which hadn't left her hand since she arrived, to snap a picture of his without asking. She began silently typing with a sardonic expression.

"You still have that?" Ruth asked.

"Of course," he said.

She nodded like she shouldn't be surprised.

Adam raised his eyebrows. "You might as well have a flip phone."

Gabriel shook his head, but the timer in the kitchen signaled lunch before he could explain his choice. Ruth knew. He'd only gotten a cell phone in the first place to keep in touch with her. She'd assumed he would get the oldest style phone he could find. But flip phones still had their place, whereas he felt the slide out keypad better captured a moment in time. Plus, it was a lot easier to text with. He did have a practical side.

Mrs. Ziebert was the first into the kitchen. She silenced the timer and began calling out orders to the younger people on setting the tables and getting things out of the fridge to have lunch ready. She led her husband and Gabriel's parents into the dining room and left the others to fend for themselves in the kitchen. Everyone filled a plate and took a seat.

Maybe it was only because they'd just been talking about phones, but Gabriel noticed that the phones matched up the pairs at the table. Adam and Kayla had theirs on the table in near constant use during the meal. He suspected they were texting each other from a foot away. Isaac and Jessica had their phones out, but they were face down on the table and mostly left alone.

Ruth's phone was not in sight. Gabriel wanted to ask her about it. He wanted to ask and didn't want to ask if he'd been deleted from her phone. How long had it taken her? Was there any way to go back? Or start over?

He mostly made small talk with Isaac instead, who he also hadn't seen in a while. He asked when the baby was due and where he was working. Ruth and Jessica added to the pleasant chat. The food disappeared while they talked. Isaac and Jessica moved into the dining room to chat with the parents as soon as they cleared their plates.

The engaged couple was still absorbed in virtual reality at the other end of the table. Ruth seemed to be growing more tense now that she was left alone – so to speak – with Gabriel.

"Should I get those books?" he suggested.

"Yes," she said. "This is probably a good time to get to work."

He brought the two library books from the living room. Ruth had moved both of their plates to the counter to make room. He set the books between them as he reclaimed his chair. "Any ideas on what saint you'd like to start with?"

She sighed a sigh that was almost a groan. "Nobody I don't know."

"You want to start with the more famous names?"

"No, those are the ones I don't know."

"You lost me."

Ruth smiled, looking satisfied that she'd confused him. Then she opened the top book to the table of contents and spoke more seriously. "Look, I've never really been into saints. I haven't studied them. If we pick one of these names that *everyone* knows, there will be someone in the room who knows a whole lot more than me. I don't want to look like an idiot."

"You won't look like an idiot no matter who we pick," Gabriel said. "We're not teaching a class, we're... facilitating a discussion."

"Yeah, well, I don't want to facilitate a discussion about how much I don't know."

Gabriel was still thinking about what she'd said earlier. "You may have a point though."

She tipped her head and narrowed her eyes somewhat threateningly. "About how much I don't know?"

A girl didn't grow up with three older brothers without really thick skin. Gabriel knew that as well as he knew Ruth knew that wasn't what he meant. He smiled at her expression and said, "If we discuss some of the quote unquote major saints, there will probably be some people who already know a lot and some who don't. Discussing more obscure saints might sort of... level the playing field and make everyone more comfortable."

Adam looked up from his phone. "Yeah, sis, it's not just about you."

She rolled her eyes at him and then scanned the names in the contents of the book in front of her. "Hmm... I've never heard of this one. How about Catherine of Siena?"

"You've never heard of Catherine of Siena?" Gabriel gaped at her. He thought she was joking and played along. "She's got to be one of the most well-known mystics and one of I think not too many women to be named a Doctor of the Church."

Ruth had evidently been serious because she glared at him and said, "Stop showing off, Batman."

"Hey, what are you going to call this group anyway?" Adam asked suddenly.

Since Gabriel was still trying to pull his foot out of his mouth, he was going to let Ruth answer. "Do we need a name?"

She shook her head. "The group doesn't need a name, Adam. It doesn't need a secret handshake either."

"What?" Adam feigned shock. "I was only going to come for the secret handshake."

"No," Ruth said, "you're going to come because of your burning interest in..." She ran her finger up and down the list as she turned to Gabriel. "Which of these saints do you know the least about?"

He picked the first unfamiliar name he saw. "St. Marianne Cope?"

Ruth looked at her brother. "You know you've always wanted to learn about St. Marianne Cope."

"Fascinating," he said dryly. His phone pinged and his eyes returned to it.

Mrs. Ziebert walked into the room carrying a stack of plates. Isaac was behind her with more. "Did I hear that my daughter knows nothing of St. Catherine?"

"Not nothing," Ruth said. "I know that she was a mystic and a Doctor of the Church."

Her mom smirked at the answer before she shook her head sadly. "Your faith formation teacher did a terrible job."

Ruth laughed.

Gabriel understood the joke because Mrs. Ziebert had been

Ruth's faith formation teacher – as well as his – all through elementary school.

The dishwasher rattled as Isaac pulled out a rack for the dishes he carried. "Mom," he said, "you need Baby Ruth in your class this year, not as a helper but as a first grader." Then he shot his sister a look that dared her to retaliate.

"Oh, yeah," she said. "What do you know about St. Marianne Cope?"

"Nothing yet," Isaac said. "But I plan to read up on her this week so I can make you look bad on Friday."

Ruth stood up. "You would totally do that, wouldn't you?" She picked up the books. "Come on, Gabe. We're going to pick a new saint and not tell anyone who it is before Friday."

As Gabriel followed her from the room, he heard Isaac mumble something about knowing who was really in charge. It wouldn't matter to Gabriel if he was the sidekick. If they could figure out how to be a good team again, he'd be happy to spend time with Ruth and whatever saint she wanted.

6

Nerves sprang to life as Mrs. Donnelly opened the door. Ruth had been waiting in front of the school for ten minutes, feeling very prepared. Once Mrs. Donnelly arrived with the keys and let her into first the building then the teachers' lounge, Ruth began to wish she was still waiting. She wasn't prepared at all.

"You're welcome to move things around," Mrs. Donnelly said, "but it has to go back just like this when you're done."

Ruth nodded her understanding. She'd never been in a teachers' lounge. The space felt off-limits and intimidating even as Mrs. Donnelly motioned her into the room.

"I'll be back at 8:30 to lock up." Mrs. Donnelly peered over her glasses, asking her if there was anything else she needed.

She needed Gabriel. Why wasn't he there yet? Ruth nodded at Mrs. Donnelly though. "We'll make sure we finish on time."

The older woman patted her arm. "You'll be fine," she said. Then she left.

Ruth stood inside the doorway wondering how it was going to be fine. The feeling was as crippling as it was sudden. She hadn't been worried all week. She and Gabe picked a saint. He was going to read a few paragraphs on that saint and then she would ask the questions. There were only three relevant questions in the book, but that had seemed like plenty on Sunday. Most of the members would know each other. They didn't really need to stay on topic the whole time. She figured a few questions would get them started. Then they'd just let people talk until it was time to clean up.

Doubts overwhelmed Ruth as she faced the actual meeting space. The room was so large and quiet. There were four round tables. How could they talk if a bunch of people had their backs to each other? Ruth pulled out her phone and snapped a picture to help her remember how the furniture started. She tipped one of the tables to its side to fold in the legs. Her fingers were shaking, but she needed to make herself do something other than think about how bad it could be. She planned to set all the tables against the wall. She'd only pushed in two legs when Gabe walked in.

"Hi," he said as he rushed over to help with the other legs. He took the table from her. "Where do you want this?"

"I thought we'd stack them against that wall." Ruth pointed. She put her hand down quickly to hide the trembling.

Gabe rolled the table to where she'd pointed as he said, "Glad I'm not the only one who's nervous."

A rush of gratitude came when he noticed her shaking hands. She was glad he was there. Tension over the missed years was still palpable in the room, but wonderful memories were there as well. Ruth remembered the way Gabe used to quiz her over the phone the night before a test. He made silly sound effects for right and wrong answers, sometimes so silly that she had to ask which was which. She remembered how they used to leave funny notes to each other in their instrument cases in the band room and how they'd passed out candy together on Halloween three years in a row.

Ruth had been so annoyed when she saw Gabe's name in that email from Mrs. Donnelly and yet she knew none of the other people she'd considered would have given her the peace she felt having him there now. Whatever was or wasn't going on between them personally, Gabe was smart and dependable and there to help.

"Do you want me to help with that one or fold another one?" he asked.

"Uh..." Ruth had just gotten a second table on its side. "Can you do that one?" As happy as she was to have his help, she still wanted a little distance. She was feeling attracted to Gabe on top of the gratitude and awkwardness. There was a whole casserole of emotions she needed to keep on the back burner while she focused on simply being nervous about the meeting.

He nodded and went to work. He had both the other tables folded and against the wall about the same time she finished hers. They stood side by side looking at the chairs that had been shoved into a mess to get the tables out of the way. Without speaking, they began to arrange those chairs into a big circle. The legs scraped loudly on the hard floor as they were slid around the room. Isaac and Jessica came in while they were working.

"Making enough noise, Baby Ruth?"

"Almost. Did either of you get some friends to come?" She'd asked all of her brothers to come and invite friends. She'd been working on Ella, who was surprisingly reluctant after saying not too long ago that she'd like to join a group like this.

Jessica shook her head.

Isaac said, "Sebastian said he'd come."

The room became incredibly quiet as Ruth and Gabe stopped pushing chairs. Gabe recovered first and got the last few chairs lined up. Ruth stared at her brother for a moment. She didn't know what to say. She worried that Sebastian's presence would make everyone uncomfortable but knew that was a terribly uncharitable attitude. And it wasn't as though he could be uninvited anyway. Maybe if they had enough people, it'd be easier to ignore him.

Ruth turned to Gabe. "Is Eric coming?"

He shrugged.

"Didn't you ask him?"

"I, uh..."

"Hi." A chipper female voice interrupted as someone new entered the room.

Ruth smiled to greet her. She was familiar and Ruth knew she'd been in Adam's class but was having trouble recalling her name. Then Adam and Kayla walked in right behind her. The first woman was evidently a friend of Kayla's because the two of them claimed chairs next to each other and began to jabber away. Adam took the chair on Kayla's other side while staring at his phone.

Sebastian Jones came in next and walked up to Isaac, who greeted him with a handshake. Ruth moved a little closer to Gabe and pulled out her phone to text Ella. She replied that she'd decided to skip the first meeting. Two other young women had sat near Kayla when Ruth looked up again. They were huddled together whispering, and Ruth could sense by the furtive glances that Sebastian was the subject.

Gabe had taken a seat. He was flipping through the book of saints. It made Ruth almost smile to see his nervousness. She knew he had the page bookmarked and that he was only putting on a show of finding the right page to look busy. She had the questions on her phone and made sure they were ready to pull up, also to look busy.

Another young woman entered the room. This one was not one of Kayla's friends because she stopped inside the doorway and looked around uncertainly. Ruth stepped over to introduce herself. Then she realized that nametags would have been a good idea. The newcomer, Julia, followed Ruth into the circle.

Ruth sat next to Gabe and Julia sat on her other side. Ruth

looked around the circle. There were eleven people, including her and Gabe, which was not a bad turnout. It still bugged her that a few of the people she expected were not there. She'd talk to Ella later. She turned to Gabe and whispered, "Where's Eric?"

He only shrugged again in response.

Joseph had to be up at 2 AM so at least he had a good excuse.

"Are we ready to start?" Isaac asked.

Ruth glanced at the clock and at Gabe. It was a few minutes after seven. They probably should start. Gabe gave a subtle sign that he would be the one to begin the meeting.

He drew in a full breath before he spoke loudly. "Hi, everyone. Thanks for coming. I think most of you already know that I'm Gabriel and this is Ruth."

Ruth gave a quick wave to acknowledge her introduction.

"I thought we'd open with a prayer," Gabe continued. "That seems appropriate for a church group." He started the Our Father and everyone joined in. Then he paused. Ruth wasn't sure if it was an intentional moment of silence or merely Gabe trying to decide what to say next. She glanced around the room and saw several people looking at him as though it was the latter.

He cleared his throat. "We're going to discuss St. Serapion tonight."

There was a brief but unmistakably derisive snicker from one of Kayla's friends at the name.

Gabe continued as though he didn't notice. He opened his book and read several facts about the saint's life. Then he gestured that he was turning the figurative mic over to Ruth.

She tried to smile at everyone. "Uh, okay. So Gabe read the quote from St. Serapion about how all of God's creatures have a... a use or a purpose. We thought we could talk about some of the animals we tend to think of as nuisances. Bees come to mind. I mean, most of us are afraid of getting stung but they do help us pollinate lots of... um, plants. Lots of food we like we might not have if we didn't have bees to help." Ruth realized as she stopped how fast she'd been talking. She looked around the room for someone to pick up the question she'd dropped rather ungracefully. She'd talked too fast to even remember if there was a question in what she'd said.

"Well..." Isaac turned some attention his way while he thought. He glanced affectionately at Jessica. "I know my wife hates spiders, but they are a good food source for birds."

"The birds that leave droppings all over my car, no doubt." One of the trio next to Kayla said it. The others gave nods of agreement.

"What use are birds anyway?" another one asked. It was clearly a rhetorical question meant to be funny.

Adam was still holding his phone in front of his eyes. "Chicken does taste good," he said.

There were a few chuckles.

Ruth was panicking though. This was not the direction the conversation was supposed to take. "How about bacteria?" she asked. She'd made herself a mental list to have examples ready but wanted to see if anyone else would mention the benefits first.

No one said anything for a while. Then one of Kayla's increasingly obnoxious friends held up a foot and said, "I know what alligators are good for." She waved her sandal expecting admiration.

"The bad bacteria does probably come to mind before the good," Gabe said. He looked at Isaac. "Are mosquitos food for birds, too?"

Isaac smiled. "Maybe birds are the most useful creatures around because of what they eat."

Jessica nodded and put her hand in his.

"Bird watching is a hobby for some people," Sebastian observed.

Total silence met his comment. Isaac nodded, but it was clear the four women setting the negative tone felt that speaking after Sebastian Jones was as bad as speaking to him.

"Okay," Ruth said, "next question. In recognizing how important all of God's creation is..." It was something they hadn't actually done but should have happened after the last question. "How can we take care of it? Or what specifically do you do or try to do to be good stewards of the earth?" Ruth blew out a breath at the end of the question that felt wrong on every level. They'd thought when they picked the question that something nice and broad would open up tons of discussion. But with the current mood, it felt like asking for a dissertation from a kindergartner.

And at first, that was exactly the response it produced. Blank stares.

"This is a question about living simply, isn't it?" Adam said eventually. "Does it count if I live simply out of financial necessity?"

"I drive a Prius. It's brand new."

"Me, too! Car twins!"

Two of Kayla's friends bumped shoulders at this proclamation.

Ruth had planned to bring up how she packed her lunch in reusable containers four days a week. But she couldn't say it. It felt as though she'd either be bragging about the effort or pointing out the one day a week she did *not*.

"Well, I walk whenever I'm going somewhere in town," Gabe said. "But I admit I do that mostly because it feels like a hassle to move my car three or four blocks. How much does intent count?"

He was trying to make eye contact with Adam, who was oblivious and staring at a tiny screen in front of him.

"That's interesting," Isaac said. "I think the benefit is there whether you intend it or not. I worry more about the opposite. Sometimes I intend to be better but let the hassle stop me."

"Do you care to elaborate?" Gabe looked pleased by the possibility of deeper discussion.

Isaac appeared thoughtful, as though he was happy to share and trying to come up with a good example.

Jessica took over for him. "One thing we've talked about is getting some local produce from the farmers market. But then I'm at Seymour's and it's like... I'll just get apples here and save myself a trip."

"My mom and I live just outside town so we don't have trash pickup," Sebastian said. "It's a hassle to take the trash and recycling to different places so I usually don't bother. I've been intending to do better."

Gabe added a green failure of his own. Ruth noticed that Kayla and her friends appeared to be texting each other while sending not as covert as they thought glances at Sebastian.

The discussion actually continued for a while, switching to more positive efforts. Julia had a few good points. Ruth did eventually share her lunch routine. All in all, the evening might not have been too bad for a first meeting.

Except that there were five people on one side of the room absorbed in their own world and occasionally giggling over things in it while the other side of the room tried to carry on a conversation. The unspoken conflict added to Ruth's emotional casserole and threatened to overflow. All she kept thinking was that she was mostly talking to Isaac and Jessica and she could do that every Sunday in a more comfortable setting without having to do homework first.

When there was a lull at 8:15, she told everyone they needed to reorganize the room for Mrs. Donnelly rather than mention the third question. Julia and Sebastian quietly slipped from the room. Adam and Isaac helped Gabe put the tables back while Jessica helped Ruth get the chairs around them. Ruth checked the picture to see that they got it right while most of the others left. She knew Kayla's friends were still talking about Sebastian because she heard phrases like, "can't believe he was here," and "should be in jail."

The room appeared to be just as it had started.

"A little rough in the beginning," Isaac said, "but I think we're off to a promising start." He and Jessica, besides Gabe, were the only ones still there.

"Are you kidding?" Ruth asked. "Which meeting were you at? That was a disaster."

"It wasn't a disaster." Jessica stretched out the last word, trying to say it only partly described the evening.

Ruth widened her eyes skeptically. Even a partial disaster was pretty bad.

"Kayla's friends were a little..." Jessica pressed her lips together for a moment. "Anyway, I bet they only came to see if any single guys were here so they won't be back."

"Thanks," Gabe said flatly.

"I mean..." Jessica's eyes darted around the room for help.

"I think she means because they outnumbered the guys," Ruth said.

Jessica nodded.

"Don't worry," Isaac said. "It's gonna get better. Joseph said he can come next week."

"If it's just the family, we might as well talk at Mom and Dad's."

"Come on, Baby Ruth." Isaac looked serious and mature even for twenty-nine. "What about Julia? And Sebastian? And Gabriel? I think this group could be important for some people."

"Then why don't you lead it?" Ruth challenged. She was still agitated.

Isaac smiled. "Mrs. Donnelly didn't ask me." He took Jessica's hand and they waved as they moved towards the door. "See you next week. And on Sunday."

Ruth didn't say goodbye. She was fuming at him for looking so relaxed. She felt a tap as Gabe poked the corner of a book into her arm to get her attention.

"Do you want to plan when to pick a saint for next week?" he asked, somewhat timidly.

"I'm not doing this again."

"I think Isaac's right," Gabe said. "I think we just need to persevere for a bit. It'll get better."

Ruth shook her head. She wanted out of that room. "I quit," she said. "You're going to have to be Batman *and* Robin." She walked out, feeling a sting from her conscience for quitting on him and leaving him to wait for Mrs. Donnelly alone. It wasn't quite enough to make her turn around though.

7

There was a line of antique books on Gabriel's shelf that he never intended to read. He'd never been closer to opening one than he was the next Saturday evening. He was just sitting there wishing his phone would buzz and thinking he could distract himself with an Agricultural Report from 1881. It was lunacy to think corn production would make him less inclined to climb the walls, but that was how things were looking.

In the past, Ruth had usually needed a little time to become rational again when she got upset. Gabriel hoped that was still the case. Not necessarily the part about needing time but the part about becoming rational again. He let her quit and walk away the previous night. Now he was devoting his whole day, possibly weekend, to convincing her to change her mind. The effort would be well worth it if she'd give some indication that it was working.

It might not be more interesting than the old Agricultural Report, but at least his message history didn't smell like musty paper. He went to the beginning of the day and read through all his texts to Ruth.

Are you ready to change your mind about quitting?

I think I'll screw this up if I have to do it myself.

Are you sure you want to quit after one meeting? Don't you want to prove we can do better?

He'd gotten no response to those texts. At that point, he'd decided to pretend she was going to keep working with him. He began to make suggestions, hoping one would either spark her interest or convince her that he wasn't qualified to continue alone.

I think I found a good one. St. Dunston. We can talk about the difference between rest and sloth.

There's something here about St. Brigid and the need for both physical and spiritual exercise. Is that a good topic?

Maybe we don't have to talk about a particular saint. How about relics in general and how some keepsakes are sort of like personal relics?

That last one is no good. It might be too personal for a group that's just starting anyway.

I know you said no common saints but what about Patrick? We can discuss how there's so much more than green beer. Did you know his given name was Maewyn?

If we're still meeting in December, we have to study St. Wenceslas. Never knew these lyrics. Thither. Yon. Knowst. It's awesomely old school. Plus, two saints in the first line.

Are you going to join the new group I got roped into leading?

That text had been sent to Eric. Gabriel wasn't thrilled about including his brother in his attempts to get Ruth back in. He didn't know how things had ended between them or even how long they had dated. But Ruth wanted Eric to come. She'd made that clear by repeatedly asking about him. What if she was still carrying a torch for Eric? It wasn't healthy to think about that.

Gabriel moved on to the rest of the texts to Ruth. He read through them wondering when his strategy changed to trying to annoy her into unquitting.

New idea. We talk about how there's a patron saint for everything. Anthony for lost things. Nicholas for children. And so on.

St. Blaise is the patron of sore throats and St. Clare for eye diseases? Everything.

Probably shouldn't talk about Jude and lost causes. Might get ugly considering our parish name.

There's a patron saint of people who work with explosives. Go St. Barbara!

I'm reading that the elders in Revelation are the saints in heaven worshipping God. It's interesting but not really a discussion starter.

Superstitions. I just had a brainstorm about talking about the danger of letting devotion to a saint lead to superstition.

Maybe we just need to put a bunch of names in a hat? Or take requests?

The messages were an accurate recap of Gabriel's day, reading about saints and bothering Ruth. It was nearly 7 PM. He dropped his phone on his kitchen table and went in search of a distraction he could eat. He didn't feel like cooking so he just put some oatmeal in the microwave. He sat down with the bowl, poking his spoon around while the contents cooled off.

A tiny red flash caught his eye. The phone had apparently buzzed while he was watching something boil. Intense disappointment flashed when he saw that the message was from Eric.

Fridays, right? Guess I might check it out.

Gabriel held the phone for a moment, thinking. He really wanted to hear from Ruth, but maybe it wasn't completely bad that he hadn't. At least she hadn't asked him to stop texting. Maybe she was still paying attention. Maybe it was time to issue an ultimatum, a very soft ultimatum, just enough to let him know if he had hope of convincing her.

Can you come over tomorrow afternoon to plan in person? BTW, Eric said he might come next time.

They could plan later in the week, but they'd talked on Sunday last time. Gabriel didn't know what other times she might have free. Plus, now the deadline for responding was close.

Not close enough. He was scraping out the last bite of oatmeal and still hadn't heard back. Considering that she'd been ignoring him all day, it shouldn't have been surprising to not get an immediate response. He'd talked himself into expecting one anyway. In fact, he'd talked himself into expecting a positive response.

He took his bowl to the sink, trying to outrun the frustration of not knowing anything. He put some water in the bowl to make it easy to wash later. Then he decided to just wash it right away. He couldn't be still. He couldn't be inside at all. The run he intended to take later in the evening, when it was cooler, was calling him outside.

Gabriel stuffed his keys in the pocket of his shorts. He reached for the phone but stopped himself. He never took anything besides keys with him on a run. Empty pockets were more comfortable. Sometimes he even left his door unlocked to leave the keys at home. Today would be no different. Just because there was a chance that Ruth was coming back into his life didn't mean he had to start acting like a lovesick teenager. He had more self-control than that. He could wait until he returned to find out if she'd been won over.

The run was pretty normal as much as it was ever normal. Gabriel didn't have a standard route. He ran around Andauk like a man looking for the lost dog he didn't have. He ran up and down streets mostly following whims but stayed close enough to home to head back when he got tired.

Ruth's parents lived within half a mile. Sometimes he happened to pass their house. The fact that he didn't that day felt deliberate. It annoyed him that there was no way around that intentional feeling. Ruth was so much on his mind that he couldn't be unaware of where she lived. He had to either run past it on purpose or not run past it on purpose.

It had probably dipped below 80 but the sun was strong, and he was certainly in need of a shower by the time he got home. He could have taken a moment to check his phone first. Not doing it felt like trying to prove something. He didn't know what he was trying to prove so he gave up delaying and made a beeline for the kitchen table as soon as he was clean and dressed. He could see the light flashing.

If it was a text from his mother, who texted him more than anyone else, he would be particularly ungrateful for whatever random thought she'd shared because of the timing. Fortunately – though his mom had sent her plans for dinner the next day as a hint rather than an invitation – there was also a brief message from Ruth.

3 o'clock? Where do you live?

So short, yet so meaningful. Ruth was back in. She was going to keep leading the meetings, keep spending time with Gabriel while they planned. Asking her to come over had felt natural and familiar. But she didn't know where he lived. That was a blunt reminder of how much time had passed. Could they really begin a new friendship? And could it this time be the beginning of a whole life together?

One step at a time. Gabriel told her that 3 o'clock would work for him and sent his address. Then he looked around to see if anything needed to be done to his place before 3 o'clock.

****

Ruth arrived about ten minutes after three. Gabriel hadn't been watching the clock. He only knew what time she arrived because he happened to check the time right before she knocked. And maybe a few other times.

The first thing she said when he opened the door was, "Sorry I'm late."

"You're not late," Gabriel said. "This isn't a dentist

appointment or... I hope it's not as unpleasant at least."

"I like my dentist." Ruth smiled, showing naturally straight teeth. She hadn't had braces like he had. "And I've still never had a filling."

"That's why you like your dentist. Still... 3 o'clock wasn't a strict appointment time."

She smiled vaguely. Her expression was about as inspired as the conversation as she glanced past him.

"Oh, yeah. Come on in." Gabriel stepped back to let her through the door. She smelled like baby powder as she walked past, which was a scent he didn't particularly like except that it reminded him of Ruth.

She was wearing a light blue dress with varying length ruffles that fell just past her knees. It was very pretty. He mostly liked it because he knew she'd put it on for church that morning. The previous week, when she'd been surprised to see him, she'd changed out of her nice clothes. He wondered if she'd kept the dress on this week to look nice for him. She probably hadn't. The dress probably had nothing to do with him. The possibility that it did still tickled his pride.

"So how long have you lived here?" Ruth asked.

Gabriel got his head off possibilities and back to the present. "Since January," he said. "I stayed with my parents for a while after I graduated. Uh, do you want a tour?"

Her eyes darted around the room uncertainly. She was holding a small purse and twisting the straps around her wrist. "I... I guess."

Was she nervous or simply wishing she was somewhere else? "Okay." Gabriel looked around, observing how little there was to say about his place. "That's a bedroom." He pointed to a door that was closed because he'd thrown a few things in there to make the rest of the apartment look clean. "There's a bathroom there and another tiny bedroom that, uh..." He gestured to the doorway because a quick look would capture the nothingness better than he could describe it.

There was a treadmill in the middle of the room, a few hand weights, a really old desk, and several lamps sitting on the floor in a corner that his parents had insisted he needed. Ruth poked her head in the room and backed out again with an unimpressed nod.

"Kitchen obviously." Gabriel continued the tour with a wave towards a few cabinets. "And then we're back to where we started."

Ruth stepped back to the main room. It looked as though she was about to shrug when her eyes landed on something and froze. A slow smile bloomed as her arms relaxed, no longer twisting the purse strap. "Oh," she said, "you still have it."

"Of course I still have it," Gabriel said. "That's my most prized possession." It was a wood covered stereo that used to belong to his grandparents. They'd given it to him when he was ten.

"I know." Ruth walked towards the old stereo. "I'm just happy to see it." She ran her hand lightly along the edge of the lid. "We had so much fun with this thing," she said. "Can I open it?"

"Sure." He came close enough to see inside as she lifted the lid on its hinge. A row of silver buttons turned it on and switched it from radio to record player to 8-track player. The power button clicked and hummed as he brought the cabinet speakers to life. "What do you want to listen to?"

"Does the 8-track still work?"

"As much as ever." The thing had been temperamental at least as long as it'd been in Gabriel's custody.

Ruth was flipping through the tapes – all of which used to belong to his grandparents as well – and making memory-triggered faces at each one. Her smile got bigger and smaller as the thoughts flickered across her face. She paused and let out a laugh at a tape of kids' songs. "Remember how much Eric used to hate this one?"

"I remember how he acted like he hated it."

"He would run screaming from the room if I even suggested I was going to play it. So funny because it was so unlike him otherwise." Ruth paused to enjoy the memory. Then she picked up the Boston tape. "The dance," she said. "Every time we heard *Peace of Mind* that dance just... It was the stupidest thing."

"It was fun. Why did we ever stop doing that?" Gabriel remembered the dance well. His parents had come in when the song was playing once and broke into a spontaneous dance. They put both hands up with their fingers laced and swayed.

Gabriel and Ruth had both thought it looked silly. They'd been about fourteen and laughed. Then they started copying the move. It had been intended as mocking, but before long they did that dance every time the song come on and for months.

"I believe you said we were starting to look as bad as your parents." Ruth put the tape in the stack of those she'd already looked through. "I'm kind of surprised your parents let us listen to that in the first place. Some of those songs are a little... inappropriate."

"We were in high school," Gabriel said.

"Yeah. And *Christmas with the Chipmunks* was still my favorite." She waved that tape. "So it isn't surprising that those other songs went over my head."

"You always skipped the Dave songs."

"I don't think I really had anything against him. I just liked pushing the buttons." She mimed poking at a button with a satisfied smirk.

Gabriel remembered that, too. He didn't let anyone else

touch his stereo. But he trusted Ruth to push all the buttons she wanted.

"Oh, I found it." Ruth had finished the 8-tracks and flipped a record around to show him the cover. "Time to admit you actually like this one."

"I admit nothing."

"Come on, you were always like, 'Let's play this one for my dad because he likes it.' I don't think you were that nice. I think this was secretly your favorite record." She pulled *Good Old Country Gospel* out of its sleeve while she was talking and slipped it onto the player as though it hadn't been years.

"You never put up much of a fuss when I got it out," Gabriel countered. "Maybe it was secretly *your* favorite."

Ruth scrunched up her nose as she put the needle in place and adjusted the volume. "Definitely not my favorite. But I never minded it, and it's pretty calm. It'll be good background music so we can get to work."

Right. She was only there because Mrs. Donnelly had cornered her. Gabriel needed to focus on the sad truth that Ruth was only spending time with him to work on their church assignment if he had any hope of making that a temporary truth. They had to make the next meeting go well enough that she wanted to continue. Then maybe he could work on getting to spend time with her for other reasons. "You're right," he said. "We should get to work." He motioned her to his tiny kitchen table where he'd left some books and a laptop.

"You were throwing out a lot of ideas yesterday," Ruth said as she took a seat. "Which one do you feel strongest about today?"

He shrugged and pushed a book towards her. "I marked a few promising pages. You tell me what looks good."

She opened to the first bookmark and began to read. After a

minute, she moved to the next page he'd marked without comment on the first. She flipped through the book looking thoughtful and then, very quietly, began to sing along with the record.

He tried to pretend he didn't notice. She would never sing in front of him on purpose, but there was something about that album. She couldn't seem to stop herself from singing along without realizing it. That was why it had secretly been one of his favorites and why he hadn't listened to it in years.

Ruth had a few good ideas. She'd apparently been giving the matter some thought while she was not responding to his texts. They took some notes and made progress on their plan for Friday. Ruth was singing again as he wrote out a question they wanted to use. She stopped in the middle of a line.

Gabriel looked up because he thought she'd stopped to say something. Her head was down. She was biting her lower lip and blushing. "You don't have to stop," he said. "It sounds nice when you sing."

"I don't sing in front of anyone."

Time to break it to her gently. "You always sang with this record."

"No, I..." Ruth's eyes moved around the table between them and didn't meet his. "I know I used to, but I always thought I caught myself before you noticed or was too quiet to hear."

He shook his head. "I heard you." He wanted to reiterate how nice her voice sounded, tell her how much he'd always liked it. But something stopped him. The memory seemed too intimate to share with the awkwardness of lost time still between them. Besides, it should have been obvious that he didn't mind her singing or he wouldn't have played the record so often.

Ruth had her lips pinched together. It looked as though she might have been deciding whether or not to let herself sing. If she'd been considering it, she must have decided firmly against it because she got up, carrying a book with her finger marking the page, and turned off the music. She returned to the table looking either sad or angry – maybe both – and said, "It'll be easier to concentrate this way."

Gabriel nodded even though he disagreed. He found it much harder to concentrate with the silence. It pressed on him with the knowledge that he'd offended Ruth in some way. It was wrong to tell her the truth about her singing. Honesty was supposed to be important though. He tried to do the right thing. She was probably upset that it'd taken so long. He couldn't undo that. At least she wasn't too angry to do their homework. She seemed to have no trouble concentrating on saints and nothing else.

8

"Ruth's here!" Ella's voice called out as soon as Ruth opened the office door.

Mr. Sweet popped out of his office at the same time. He looked panicked.

There was a clear sense that the two of them had been waiting on her. Ruth wasn't late though. She dropped her bag on her desk and turned from father to daughter to see which one would tell her why they seemed to be pouncing.

"My printer isn't working," Mr. Sweet said.

"I can't fix printers."

"You always say that," Ella said, "and then you always fix it."

Ruth sighed and went into Mr. Sweet's office. Always was an exaggeration, if not strictly false. They'd gotten a new printer about six months earlier that gave them a lot of trouble. Ruth had cleared several paper jams and reconnected a cable that had come loose. She'd never actually *fixed* a printer. But for some reason both Ella and Mr. Sweet seemed reluctant to touch the new printer so Ruth was left to try fiddling with it when there was trouble.

"Did it start and then stop?" she asked, which would mean something was likely jammed.

"No, it's not doing anything." Mr. Sweet gestured Ruth towards the printer but kept himself well away from it, either to give Ruth room to work or because he was afraid it might start spraying toxic gas.

Ruth doubted he thought anything like that. The image made her smile as she opened the back though. No stuck paper. She prodded the cables to make sure everything was secure. Then she turned it off, counted to three, and turned it back on. She stepped to Mr. Sweet's computer to make sure there was something in the queue because she was running out of ideas. The printer sprang to life as she was reaching for the mouse.

"Thank you," Mr. Sweet said, looking relieved.

Ella was cheering from the next room.

"You're welcome," Ruth said. "I just turned it off and on. You could try that next time."

He shook his head. "Probably wouldn't work for me. It likes you."

She went back to her own desk. There was no denying that it felt good to be appreciated even if she was appreciated for something that wasn't really a skill. A random thought popped into her head. "I wonder if there's a patron saint of printers or people who fix printers."

Ella chuckled softly. "That's kind of funny. But I'm afraid it's your segue into yelling at me for not coming on Friday."

That hadn't been Ruth's line of thinking. Now that Ella brought it up though, she asked, "Why didn't you come?"

"I was going to." Ella tipped her head with a guilty expression. "I don't know why I... I just chickened out at the last minute."

"Well, you didn't miss much. I totally bombed as a leader."

"Oh, no. I'm sorry."

"Joseph wasn't there either."

"Hmm." Ella attempted to sound disinterested with a glance towards her father's office. Her cheeks turned a bit pink. "What makes you think you bombed?"

Ruth tried to shrug. She knew why though. "I didn't take it seriously enough. Gabriel and I just threw out a couple of questions, and I didn't know what to do or... I just wasn't prepared. But... I think it'll be better this week."

"All right, ladies." Mr. Sweet came through his door stuffing a folder into his briefcase. "I'm going to be out all morning. I'll call to check in at least once."

"We got it, Dad."

He made his way out the door with a few final instructions.

Ruth settled in for a Monday morning.

Ella was very interested in talking while they worked. "What makes you think this Friday will be better?"

The question had a probing quality that might have gotten Ruth's defenses up. But she had a feeling it had to do with Gabriel and not her leadership skills. She wanted to talk about Gabe. She waded into the conversation carefully in case Ella's motive for asking was actually about the group. "We've already spent more time discussing our plans, and I think I learned a few things from the first disaster."

"When you say *we* spent time discussing it, you mean you and Gabriel?"

"Yeah. I was at his place for almost two hours yesterday."

Ella smiled and wiggled her eyebrows. "Ohhh. How was that?"

"We got a lot of work done."

"You know that's not what I'm asking," Ella said. "You told me last week that you two avoided a lot of the awkwardness because of all the other people at your parents' house. How was it with just you and him?" She put an arm on her desk and leaned towards Ruth.

"So weird," Ruth said. The things she wanted to share started to spill out. "I went over there prepared to be all businesslike, just talk about the church group. But then he looked really happy to see me, and I got all nervous like it was a first date or something."

"Aw." Ella tilted her head and sighed.

"That's not good," Ruth said.

"Why not?"

"Because it wasn't a date."

"Are you sure?" Ella got a slightly wicked expression. "You don't always know when you're on a date."

"You are so mean to bring that up."

"Sorry," Ella said, though she looked about as sorry as a kid getting the last cookie from the jar. "So then what happened?"

Ruth paused in her story. She wasn't upset with her friend for bringing up the embarrassing history. In fact, now that it was out in the open the mention had almost made her laugh. A few seconds delay would be punishment enough. "Okay. He showed me around a bit, and he has this old stereo that we used to play with all... the... time. His grandparents bought it like maybe in the 70s or something and eventually gave it to him because they knew he likes old stuff. It has an 8-track player and everything."

"What's an 8-track?"

"Exactly. It's *that* old. Anyway, he still had the same tapes and records, and as I looked through them it was as if we'd gone back in time. For us. It was like we were still friends and had all these great memories."

Ella nodded that she was still paying attention. She was also using her phone to look at pictures of 8-track tapes.

"For a minute," Ruth continued, "I started to think we could just forget about the missing years and pretend our relationship hadn't dissolved simply because of... stubbornness." She winced at the word that didn't feel adequate. As embarrassing as the situation had been, the knowledge that she'd given up her best friend because of it was worse.

"For a minute?" Ella asked. She had a bit of a wince of her own in anticipation that things had gone downhill.

"Yeah. We were reminiscing, and that was nice. Then I remembered this silly dance we used to do. It was something his parents did once, and we made fun of them for a long time afterwards."

"What kind of dance?"

"It was..." Ruth jumped up. "Stand up and I'll show you."

Ella stood slowly, somewhat warily.

"Put your hands up like this," Ruth said.

"All right." Ella held her hands up at shoulder height to mirror Ruth.

Ruth put their palms together and laced her fingers in Ella's. "Imagine some classic rock." She swayed and moved their hands in circles.

"This is ridiculous." Ella was watching the glass front door for anyone who might be approaching or even passing by.

"I know it is," Ruth said. She dropped Ella's hands. "But we were pretty young and sometimes something is funny just because... I don't know... just..."

"I know what you mean." Ella reached for a ringing phone. "Inside jokes," she said before it got to her ear.

Ruth nodded and looked for something to do while Ella handled the customer on the phone. Neither was busy for long before Ella returned them to the subject still in Ruth's head. "You weren't actually dancing with Gabriel yesterday, were you?" she asked.

Ruth groaned. "Not even close."

"Then why did you bring it up?"

"Because I thought about it. I was holding the tape with the song we used to dance to and... he was right there... I couldn't stop myself from picturing grabbing his hands to dance the old dance, and I could tell how different it would be without even doing it."

"Different in a good way?"

"No, but... not entirely bad either."

Ella squinted. "That's not a cryptic answer or anything."

"I'm trying to think how to describe it," Ruth said. Her mind filled with images and feelings from the previous day. She'd never noticed that the stereo had a distinctive smell until it was in front of her again. The tapes had felt so familiar in her hands. And Gabriel's presence had been the most familiar. When she thought about dancing, she wanted to hug him. For so long she'd been focused on the awful ending and not thinking about all the good times that came before. She wanted to remember, and she wanted to do the stupid dance with him one more time.

But then she'd looked at him. The real, present Gabe wasn't quite the same. Her memory told her that he was six foot to her five foot seven. The height difference seemed greater than that. Had he actually grown more in the last few years or had she forgotten how much she had to look up? His hair seemed straighter. Was it longer or shorter or had she never noticed the way it hung on his forehead? He looked basically the same and yet somehow more manly, which was a word that sort of surprised her.

Gabe ran cross country and had no interest in football. He fiddled with old technology instead of cars. He didn't embody many of the stereotypically male qualities. Yet he'd always been reliable and honest, which were characteristics that defined a real man better than any hobbies. And in the moment Ruth had considered taking his hands, she'd been fully aware of him as the young man he was more than the friend he used to be. She felt a strange longing to go back in time to when things were comfortable between them. Strange because she also wanted to try to move forward, to figure out if a new relationship was possible.

"Ruth?" Ella was still waiting for an explanation, with some impatience and some concern.

"It was different in a bad way because it completely unnerved me. I was flustered and trying to change the subject before he noticed I was turning red, but..."

Ella widened her eyes.

"I... There's something hopeful in finding myself attracted to a guy I already know is really nice and who I have to spend more time with."

"Oh," Ella said. "That does sound promising."

"Except..." Ruth sighed, and it was not the happy kind of sigh. "Well, he also laughed at me."

"What do you mean?"

"We were listening to a record while we worked. It was just quiet... in the background. And I caught myself singing along. Gabe said... He said I used to do that a lot, and I didn't know." Ruth put her face on her desk and covered it with her arm.

"Wait. I'm confused." There was plenty of confusion in Ella's voice to back up her statement. "How do you catch yourself singing and not know it?"

Ruth picked her head up enough to prop her chin on her arm. "I didn't know he knew."

"That he knew what?"

"That I used to sing along with that record. I know I was quiet, and I always thought I caught myself before he heard. But yesterday he said he had heard me."

"He heard you yesterday?"

"No. I mean, he did. But that wasn't... Well, it bothered me but not as much as..." Ruth stopped for a breath, wondering why the words were so hard to get out. "He said he'd always heard me and looked so... amused is putting it mildly. I didn't think my voice was *that* bad. I must've been singing in front of his brother and his parents. What if it was a running joke to them? What if that's even why his dad liked the record? To laugh at my singing?"

"Wow." Ella shifted a few things around on her desk while she appeared to consider what to say. She began tentatively. "So, um, are you familiar with the expression 'making a mountain out of a molehill?'"

"You think I'm overreacting?" Ruth asked. Her tone was defensive but there was already hope behind it. Part of her wouldn't mind being told she had no reason to be worked up.

"You said he looked amused," Ella said. "Doesn't that mean happy? Couldn't that just mean he had a happy memory of you? Why do you jump right to he's been laughing at you for years?"

Ruth thought about whether she'd been too sensitive and uncovered a disturbing idea. "I think... I think I have been oversensitive. I really want this to be a second chance for me and Gabe, and I think I'm trying so hard not to get my hopes up that I'm not just looking for warning signs but maybe inventing them."

"So you're saying I'm right?" Ella smiled, not gloating but almost.

"Maybe. Sort of. I wish I could relax about this. If we can get the group off the ground, Gabe and I will be seeing a lot of each other." Ruth took a deep breath in and out, demonstrating her intent to calmly dismantle that mountain. "I need to focus on the group and making that work. Then just wait to see how Gabe and I are getting along."

Ella looked suddenly worried. "You don't think he's seeing anyone else, do you?"

"I haven't heard anything. And this is a small town. Oh! His mom said something last week about how both her boys were still single."

"Hmm." Interest piqued in Ella's eyes. "Eric, too?"

"Yes. And if I'm concentrating on getting this group off the ground, that means finding some regular members who come when they say they're going to."

Ella shrank a little under Ruth's pointed look. "I'm sorry," she said. "Maybe this week."

"At least I have several more days to convince you. Because right now I need to get some work done before your dad gets back."

Ella nodded and quietly picked up something she needed to do as well.

9

After a few days and more than a few requests, Ruth decided to stop pestering Ella about coming on Friday. Her new approach was to simply tell Ella that she was coming and that Ruth would pick her up and take her to make sure of it. The arrangement worked well for both of the women. Ella wanted to go. Now she could pretend she was showing up with Ruth because Ruth was being pushy, not because it was easier to walk in with a friend. Ruth could pretend she was just looking out for Ella and not making sure she wouldn't be alone with Gabe.

Gabe wasn't alone when they got there though. Ruth pulled her car into the church parking lot and saw Gabe outside the school entrance chatting with Isaac. "Looks like Mrs. Donnelly hasn't unlocked the door yet," she observed to Ella.

"At least it's not raining." Ella glanced at the cloudy sky. "Yet," she added.

Ruth looked up as she got out of the car. The sky had darkened considerably since she left her home not fifteen minutes ago. She hoped it would go ahead and rain during the meeting and be done before they came back out. *Hey, God,* she thought, *I'd rather get rained on than have another bad meeting so if I'm asking too much...*

Ella walked up to the guys a step behind Ruth, who made a point to include her right away. "You both know Ella, right? Ella

Sweet. Gabriel Chadwick. Isaac Ziebert." She pointed to each of them as she said their names.

"I remember you from school," Gabriel said. "You were in my brother's class?"

Ella nodded.

"Didn't you... uh..." Isaac looked uncertain about something. "I know you came to my parents' house with Ruth a while back, but..."

"She was probably wearing her other glasses if you're trying to figure out what's different," Ruth said.

He nodded but didn't look convinced. "Maybe that's it."

Ella had several pairs of glasses and wore her hair up, down, straight or curly. Today she had the thin black frames with low pigtails that spilled waves over her shoulders. She always seemed uncomfortable when anyone talked about the variations in her appearance. Ruth looked at Gabe to change the subject. "Mrs. Donnelly hasn't been here yet?"

Gabriel pulled the door open. "She was," he said. "I just hadn't gotten around to, uh..." He gestured through the open door.

"My fault," Isaac said. "I got here at the same time and distracted him." He lifted a hand towards the parking lot in a greeting as he finished talking.

Ruth turned to see where the wave was directed. She saw Sebastian Jones walking across the parking lot. She didn't wave. She told herself that was only because she didn't know him as well as Isaac. It had nothing to do with the voice in her head that said their group didn't need members *that* badly. After all, she did stand with everyone else to wait for him before they went inside.

Ella lagged behind as they proceeded down the hallway, and Ruth slowed her steps to walk beside her. When the three guys were sufficiently ahead, Ella widened her eyes towards them and her lips almost soundlessly asked, "Was he here last week?"

Ruth nodded. All of them had been there, but she knew exactly who they were talking about.

"Why didn't you tell me?" Ella whispered.

"I was trying to convince you to come," Ruth whispered back. "I didn't think that information would help."

Ella said nothing. Her expression agreed wholeheartedly.

The guys were already moving chairs when they entered the room. Ruth jumped in by tipping a table sideways. Ella helped her fold in the legs. They were about to roll it to the wall when Sebastian appeared between them. He picked it up effortlessly and said, "Let me get this for you."

Ruth let go with a quiet thank you.

Ella backed up so quickly she was lucky she didn't stumble. Then she turned and put her hands on the back of a chair as though she'd been rushing to help line up the circle.

"I wish I knew how many to expect," Gabriel said thoughtfully. He was looking at the same circle of chairs.

"Let's keep it small," Ruth said. "One for each of us plus maybe two more for now, and we'll add chairs as people come." *If they come.*

There was some nodding in the group. Isaac went ahead and took a seat.

"Are either of your other brothers coming?" Ella asked. She motioned Ruth into the chair next to hers.

"I don't think so." Ruth glanced away with a flash of guilt. "Joseph was going to, but he texted me yesterday that someone asked to trade shifts with him."

Ella lifted her eyebrows in a manner that accused Ruth of withholding all kinds of pertinent information.

"I haven't specifically heard from Adam," Ruth continued,

"but... well, I've been getting vibes that he's not particularly interested." She exchanged a knowing look with Isaac, then turned to Gabe. "Hey, what about your brother?"

"Eric?" he asked, as though he had more than one brother.

"Yes, Eric. I thought you said he was going to be here."

"He told me he might come." Gabriel's tone was defensive, and he seemed to realize it. "I could text him to find out, but at this point he's either on his way or not coming. I don't think it'd make any difference."

"No, don't bother to, um..." Ruth fidgeted in her chair. It occurred to her for the first time that Gabriel could have had a falling out with his brother over the date that wasn't a date. Was that giving herself too much power? Why else would Gabe sound reluctant to include his brother?

There wasn't time to ponder any questions before Ruth sensed movement behind her. She turned to see Eric come into the room.

"Speak of the devil," Gabe mumbled.

"This looks like the right place," Eric said. He exchanged waves and greetings as he made his way to the chair on Gabe's other side. "I see why you need me. Turnout's a bit light."

"We just couldn't do without your sparkling personality," Gabe answered dryly, but with no animosity. If there had been any friction, it was in the past.

Eric nodded at the sarcastic compliment as though it was sincere. "Hi, Ella. How did Ruth talk you into coming?"

"She, um..." Ella's mouth moved quietly. She appeared to be doing some mental scrambling while her face warmed. "She drove me here."

"Ha," Isaac laughed. "You kidnapped her? That's how you get people to come to your meeting, Ba-, uh, Ruth?"

"Yes, Ike." He'd come close enough. "I kidnapped her. I also promised her Eric's sparkling personality."

The comment earned some laughter.

Gabriel said, "Let's get started. I mean, it's time to start."

It was 7 o'clock. Ruth nodded at him to begin.

He led them in what was becoming the regular prayer. Then he opened the big hardcover book on his lap and fanned through the pages, letting it fall closed again. "There are a lot of saints in here," he said. "Ruth and I were talking about which ones might be interesting for this group, and she asked me why I thought Mrs. Donnelly wanted us to talk about saints. Then we both thought that would be a good place to start this week, to ask all of you why talking about saints might be a good thing. What do you hope to learn, why are you here, and so on? Aside from..." He gestured to Eric with a hint of an eye roll.

Ruth felt herself smile along with the others at the teasing reference.

Eric tugged on his collar to be the center of attention, though he was wearing a simple blue t-shirt and not a necktie like Gabriel. "Can I say I'm here because my brother asked me to come?"

"You can start there," Gabriel said. "But why did you agree?"

"Well, I'm here because I enjoy learning," Isaac said, "particularly about our faith. There are tons of books but... I think it's easier to process and remember things when you're talking out loud. I like a good discussion."

Ruth might have felt pressure to provide that discussion if she didn't expect Isaac to be the best contributor. Heads nodded with his words. When he finished, eyes drifted back to Eric.

"I... I guess I'm still on the hook for saying why I'm here." He smiled self-consciously. "The truth is I figured most of the people here would be here to see who else was here, and we'd have that in common."

Ella and Sebastian started to talk at the same time. He nodded for her to go first.

"I was just going to say my reason is curiosity, both about the people," she glanced at Eric, "and the topics," her eyes moved to Isaac. She waved a hand at Sebastian as soon as she was done talking.

"Eric said he was looking for something in common, and that's what draws people to the saints. There are so many that... If you have a certain job or hobby, there's a saint you can look up to. If you're struggling with something, like stress or addiction, there's a saint who's been there. We can look for commonality with the people who have gone before us as well as those who walk beside us."

Ruth nodded at him. She tried to focus on the unexpected wisdom and not the tension that sprang up when he said the word addiction. "That's why there's a patron saint for everything, right?" she asked. "To make it easier to find the saints people can relate to."

"You're catching on," Isaac said.

"I guess I knew that," Ruth said. "I just hadn't thought it through."

"That's exactly what Isaac was saying." Gabriel gestured to Ruth's brother. "About how it helps to talk things out. When I was looking at a list of patron saints, the ones that jumped out at me were the ones I could connect to in some way." He paused to acknowledge Sebastian as well. "And I didn't fully appreciate that's what I was thinking at the time."

"Which saints did you find interesting?" Isaac asked. "I

mean, if you don't mind sharing, what were some of the connections you saw?"

Gabriel opened the book on his lap again, flipping through the pages more deliberately. "This guy," he said as he turned the book so the picture was facing away from himself. "He's usually drawn with an eagle shielding him from a thunderstorm – here's an example – because people turn to him when praying against bad weather. But I think I liked the image because I don't usually mind bad weather. I'm stubborn enough to go jogging whenever I want and some people – my mom mostly – give me a hard time about that. I've always thought that rain wasn't a big deal so I could picture something imaginary kind of helping me with that conclusion."

Sebastian said something about the picture that Ruth didn't hear. She was remembering a time in high school when their class went on a field trip that included a picnic lunch. There were a few tables under a shelter and a few outside it. The kids eating at the open tables had made a dash to crowd into the shelter when a sudden thunderstorm hit. She turned around as she got under the cover to realize that Gabriel hadn't moved. He was just sitting there eating in the rain. He got away with it. Because he was generally well-liked, the other kids admired him for braving the rain rather than teasing him for being weird. Ruth had tried to give him a hard time. He threatened to hug her in his sopping clothes to the delight of onlookers. The memory made her smile before she brought herself back to the present where Gabriel was turning a few more pages.

"And this guy," he said. "Honoratus. There's almost no information about him except that he's a patron of bakers. I like to make bread, and that's why I wanted to know more about him."

The next page Gabriel flipped to was St. Vincent de Paul,

whom he and Ruth had planned to discuss. Ruth appreciated the segue as he signaled to her to start the questions.

The discussion went smoothly from there. It was primarily serious but with a few good-natured laughs. Ruth was feeling about a million times better than she had the previous Friday when she began to set the tables and chairs to rights.

Sebastian had slipped out as soon as the closing prayer was over. Isaac promised to help clean up the next week as he hurried to catch up.

Gabriel found Ruth's eye as they pushed chairs in on opposite sides of a table. "Should we make Sunday afternoon our regular planning time?" he asked.

"Yes. Do you want me to come over about three again?" Then she realized she was inviting herself over. "Or you could meet me at my parents' house," she added, because inviting him to someone else's house was so much more polite.

"I'll look for you at three," he said. He smiled nonchalantly, unconcerned with who invited whom.

Ruth tried not to concern herself with details either, but she noticed several. She noticed the lines that formed on either side of his mouth. She noticed the way one side of his lower lip covered more teeth than the other. She noticed that the simple smile made her feel relaxed and hopeful. For a moment. She also noticed Mrs. Donnelly's appearance in the doorway.

"How'd it go?" the woman asked. Her question sounded encouraging, but her eyes seemed to be counting the small number of people in the room.

"Great," Gabriel said.

"Yeah." Ruth nodded at the same time. "There were a few more people here, but we didn't all need to clean up." A few was vague enough that Ruth wasn't lying. Besides, she thought six was a legitimately good start. If they had six members they could count on, they could build on that.

"Great," Mrs. Donnelly said. She surveyed the room critically as they left it. The inspection must have held up because she said nothing else before she pulled the door closed and inserted her key. "Do you need anything before I go? Book suggestions or ideas?"

"I don't think so," Ruth said.

"I wouldn't say we need anything," Gabriel added, "but I wouldn't say no to potential knowledge. If you think of any good books or resources, please pass them along."

Mrs. Donnelly nodded approvingly at the sentiment.

Ruth might have thought someone else was kissing up. Gabriel, however, made her feel immature for not saying something like that first.

Eric was already out the front door when they turned away from the teachers' lounge. Mrs. Donnelly waved as she locked the building. It was cloudy and there was lightning in the distance, but the storm still hadn't unleashed any water.

"Is he parked in front?" Ella asked with a nod to Gabriel walking away from the parking lot.

"I assume he's parked where he lives. It's only a couple houses that way."

"Oh." Ella looked at the sky. "Should we offer him a ride?"

"Uh..." Ruth glanced at Gabriel. He didn't seem to be in any hurry to avoid the coming rain. "He was just saying how he didn't mind getting wet."

Ella shrugged and moved around to the passenger side of Ruth's white compact.

"So what did you think of tonight?" Ruth asked as they buckled up.

"Good," Ella said. "I'm actually looking forward to next week."

"I'll drive anyway." Ruth was happy to have the companionship. "I'm sorry I didn't tell you Joseph wasn't coming."

"Don't worry about it." Ella sounded sincere.

"Did you, um... What do you think about Eric?"

Ella gave an exaggerated sigh. "I did. My mom is so rubbing off on me."

"You did what?"

"I did think about him. We're talking about improving our faith and in my head I'm all like... Hey, Eric is single and he's my age and he has eyes so blue you can see them across the room."

Ruth smiled at her friend's self-disgust. And at the appreciation of bright blue eyes, a trait Eric shared with his younger brother.

"That's not the worst part," Ella continued. "She's really gotten to me because... You know when Sebastian was talking about his mom? He looked at me with this slow blink or... I don't know if that's the best way to describe it, but for a couple of moments I was totally looking at Sebastian Jones like he was an eligible bachelor and not the guy who beat up his old girlfriend and that I need to stay very far away from."

Ruth had no response for that admission. If the guy was capable of abuse, Ella did need to stay away from him. But it felt unchristian to agree to avoid someone. Where exactly was the line between loving others and protecting oneself from them?

Ella was quiet for a minute as well as Ruth turned onto her street. A few raindrops plinked onto the windshield. "He and Isaac seem pretty chummy," Ella said eventually, adding another pause for prodding.

"Yeah, um... they work together. Isaac says Sebastian helped him get his current job, which he's had about two years. I don't know if he thinks he owes him something because of that or just... He defends Sebastian."

"He *defends* him?"

"Not what he did," Ruth said. She shook her head emphatically to stress that point. "Isaac has never mentioned what happened to Kathy. And it's not like we all sit around talking about Sebastian. But because they work together, his name has come up a couple of times. When there's tension or hesitation, Isaac will say something like, 'Sebastian's a good guy,' or 'People make mistakes.' Then encourage everyone to move on."

"Hmm." Ella seemed to give this some thought but was distracted by the drops falling faster and faster. "I'm about to get wet," she said. "Do you think Isaac knows about some anger management classes or just regret on Sebastian's part?"

Ruth shrugged. "Somehow I wouldn't be surprised to find out the two of them had never talked about it either. I think Isaac is just good at the whole forgive and forget thing."

"He does seem..." Ella gave an almost exasperated smile. "Don't get me wrong, I'm glad he's part of this new group. But I get the impression Isaac is going to continually make the rest of us look bad." She grabbed the door handle as Ruth's car stopped, preparing to make a run for it. "Thanks for the ride. I'll see you Monday."

Ella was out of the car and halfway to the front door while Ruth was still waving. The rain pounded on the roof of her car as she drove away.

10

There was a little old man and a little old woman who lived on Farber Road. They were both short, thin and soft-spoken, a quiet couple who had apparently been married many many years and had never had children. That seemed to be all anyone knew about them. They had somehow become famous in Andauk for being so little known.

It wasn't that Andauk was a particularly gossipy town. It was simply that most residents had lived their entire lives in that one place and had gradually developed a web of at least tenuous connections to most of the other residents. You may not know the name of the man passing on the street, but you knew he used to work at Burger Brothers. You might know the last name of the woman scanning your groceries because her husband was your soccer coach in third grade, and she looked a little like her sister, who was one of your high school teachers.

The old couple on Farber Road were outside the web. They didn't seem to be related to anyone, had never worked with anyone, just didn't seem to be known for anything besides living on Farber Road forever.

One thing that Gabriel knew about them was that they attended St. Jude's. They were there every Sunday in the middle of the pew as though saving the end for the rest of the family. Gabriel stopped in the aisle and motioned to the empty seats to ask if they were taken. The faces of the little old man and little old woman lit up as they silently indicated he was most welcome to claim a seat, which he did.

Gabriel was not avoiding his parents or trying to exert some independence when he didn't sit with them. He just liked to move around and give himself a different view now and then. After he was seated, he discovered that he'd unintentionally given himself a great view of the back of Ruth's head. She was three rows up with her dad on one side and her brother Joseph on the other. The ends of her hair were tucked between her and the back of the pew. Except for one section near her shoulder that dangled over the edge. If he'd been closer, it would have been very tempting to play with it like a soft red tassel.

Instead, Gabriel spent a lot of time watching for her to turn around. Now that they'd become friendly again, it would be perfectly natural to share a greeting. But she never turned. Even when everyone turned to their neighbors to shake hands, Ruth turned every direction besides his. Though it was possible he'd missed the opportunity when he was offering his hand to the little old couple next to him. Gabriel wished he could remember their last name.

He thought to ask them before he left, but they slipped out on his other side while the organ was still playing. Next he thought to say hello to Ruth. She hadn't moved because her parents were chatting with the people in front of them. Gabriel nodded and smiled at the few people who passed as he waited for the aisle to clear. When he had an opening, he stepped towards Ruth in time to see her wave to someone else. His eyes followed her line of sight to Eric, who waved back.

Gabriel spun around and walked out of the church. He would see Ruth soon enough.

It didn't feel soon enough even though she knocked on his door right on time. He greeted her as he'd been unable to do in the morning.

"Hi." She responded cheerfully as she entered.

She had switched to more casual clothes this week but still looked beautiful in the dark blue shirt. Gabriel loosened his tie and undid the top button under it because he remembered how she used to accuse him of making others feel shabby in comparison.

She dropped her bag on an end table. "It was very nice of you to sit with Mr. and Mrs. McGrady this morning."

McGrady. Gabriel was almost as gratified to be reminded of the couple's name as he was to find out Ruth had seen him after all. "I thought it was nice of them to save me a seat," he said. "Even if it wasn't for me specifically."

"Because you were running late?"

"No." He played along with her teasing tone. "I was almost running late. But not quite." Mostly it depended on one's definition of late for church. He'd gotten there before the first song started even if he was catching his breath as he found the page. What mattered most at the moment was that Ruth had apparently noticed when he got there. She'd noticed him before he noticed her.

"Have you given any thought to our saint of the week?"

He'd given it a lot of thought. He hoped that if they didn't need to spend much time planning the questions for Friday, they could spend some time talking more generally. "I thought maybe we could go biblical this week and study St. John the Baptist." He moved towards his kitchen table as he spoke.

Ruth followed and took the seat opposite him. "What do we like about St. John the Baptist?" she asked.

"Eating locusts. Wearing camel hair. Dunking people in the river. What is there not to like about him?"

Her laugh was the sweetest déjà vu. How many times had he said or done something to try to earn it in the past?

"I mean," she said, "why do we like him for our discussion group? Is there a topic you're attaching to him?"

"I have some ideas. But first..." He opened his laptop. "I found this video. It's aimed at kids but... Well, I thought it would be more interesting or at least different than me reading a quick bio."

"How long is it?"

"Only three or four minutes."

She nodded that he could go ahead and start the video. It seemed to entertain her, which was good. He'd been a little worried she'd say it was juvenile. "That'll be a good intro," she said when it was finished. "But then what are we going to discuss?"

"I thought he'd be a good model for talking about humility. All those people were asking if he was the Messiah. They were basically offering to worship him, and he was like 'Nah, it's not about me.' So I thought we could ask... What is the difference between true humility and false modesty? And how is humility not the same as just poor self-esteem?"

"Wow." Ruth sounded impressed. "You have definitely thought about this. Those are pretty deep questions. Did you get them from somewhere?"

She was looking at him in a way that made it difficult to focus on humility. He tried to lighten the moment. "Does my head count as somewhere?"

"What is the difference?"

"Between my head and somewhere?"

Ruth looked a lot less impressed as she clarified. "Between being truly humble and just thinking you're worthless. Every person has value, and I know God wants us to see that in ourselves. How do we balance that with... with not crossing into being prideful?"

"That's exactly what I thought we could talk about. We can ask next about what areas of our lives could use some more humility. I found this good quote." Gabriel opened a book to a marked page to make sure he said it right. "Humility is thinking about yourself less, not thinking less of yourself."

"Oh." Ruth appeared thoughtful as she absorbed the words. "So humility is not the opposite of pride at all. It's the opposite of self-centeredness."

"That's an even better way of putting it."

Ruth smiled a little deviously. "Do you think we could pretend to have this same conversation for the first time on Friday? We might actually sound sort of inspirational."

He laughed because he knew she was kidding.

"Except..." Her smile faltered. "Is self-centeredness really a word? It's kind of a mouthful."

"I think that's a word. Though you could say narcissistic instead. That's no less a mouthful but possibly more intelligent sounding. Anyway, the other question I thought of was... How does humility help with other virtues? And that one I didn't come up with by myself. There was a homily not too long ago that tied virtues to humility, and I thought it was... Going through a whole list of virtues should give us plenty to discuss."

Ruth was looking at the paper he'd used to mark his page in the book. It had questions written out as well as a few he'd crossed off. "You... uh, it looks like you had Friday already planned out before I even got here. You didn't need me to come over."

The brilliant plan to leave time to talk about non-homework topics was about to blow up in Gabriel's face. Ruth wasn't happy they were finishing quickly. She was feeling unneeded and maybe a little patronized. Her eyes darted to her purse as she was clearly thinking of collecting her things and hightailing it out of his presence.

"I did need your input," Gabriel said. He could hear desperation in his own voice and tried to calm it. "I can change any of these questions you don't like, and it's just always better to have a second opinion on... I don't want to do this by myself."

Ruth's eyes continued to avoid his. They landed on her bag again, then on the books on the table. She turned one to face her and opened it to a random page. "I suppose we could get started on next week... since I'm already here."

She wasn't leaving! "Yeah, that's a good idea. Is there a topic you'd like to discuss? Maybe we could work backwards to fit a saint to the questions."

She shrugged, flipping pages without really looking at them.

Gabriel just watched her. He sensed that he needed to back off and let her lead the conversation.

"Ew!" She jumped from the page and quickly turned it. "There are some seriously gruesome pictures in here."

"I think everyone would prefer if we stick to talking about the lives of the saints and not their deaths."

"Although some of the modern ones weren't..." Ruth trailed off. "There are still martyrs," she said quietly, "and I find that more disturbing than thinking about people who were beheaded a thousand years ago." She lifted her eyes to meet Gabriel's. "I agree we should stick to lives."

He nodded. Common ground felt wonderful. There was a moment of peace.

Ruth broke off the eye contact to return to browsing mini biographies. "I still don't... No significant connections have shown themselves to me."

"Your hero saints must be more subtle."

She squinted at him in confusion.

Gabriel wasn't exactly sure what he meant either. "Someone who is all about, say, music would immediately go to St. Cecilia, right? Maybe your personality is more complex. You need time to sift through your own dimensions before..." He stopped because she was shaking her head in disagreement but also trying not to laugh.

"It sounds like you're trying to spin my lack of distinctiveness into some sort of compliment. It's not working."

It was working. She was smiling. But Gabriel didn't argue. He tried to look as though he'd given it his best effort.

"Hey, is this the guy you mentioned on Friday?" She pointed to a page as she spun the book around to face him. "The baker?"

"Yeah."

"I was surprised when you said you liked to make bread. Is that a new hobby? I don't remember you liking to cook."

"I didn't. I mean..." He thought for a moment how to proceed. He didn't want to be too negative because they had made dinner for her family together a few times in high school. That was one of her chores, occasionally doing the cooking, and she'd enlisted Gabriel's help. "I used to be fairly indifferent to it. But that was before I needed to equip a kitchen of my own. These last few months, I've been discovering some cool... Come with me." He stood up and motioned her over to his cabinets.

"This might be my favorite." He took out several metal parts for his meat grinder to show her. "People used to grind up their own meat at home. It clamps on the counter and then I can grind up a piece of beef and imagine that I've just invented a hamburger."

Ruth appeared more amused than impressed, but she was definitely interested. Interested was good.

He opened a drawer and pulled out a spikey object attached to a wooden handle. "I don't even know what this thing is called. My mom says it's for mashing potatoes, and you know I'm not really a fan of mashed potatoes, but I used it for sweet potatoes, and it was so much more fun than a whisk or something."

"What do you have that makes bread fun?" Ruth asked.

"Excellent question." Gabriel opened a different cabinet and picked up a mortar and pestle.

Ruth's eyebrows went up. "Didn't we use something like that in chemistry?"

"A smaller one, yes."

"And how is chemistry related to bread?" She looked wary, but still amused.

"I put oats in here and crush it into oat flour."

"And that's better than just buying oat flour?"

"Of course." An idea popped into his head, related to the fact that bread took hours to make. "Do you want to try it?"

Ruth actually looked tempted. "What else do you use?"

"A dough hook." He showed her another fun tool. It looked something like a coat hanger that had been through a garbage disposal.

"My mom has something she calls a dough hook," Ruth said. "It attaches to the mixer and doesn't look much like that. I'm not sure she's ever used it."

"An electric mixer?" He made a playfully scoffing sound. "That's like letting someone else do the work and have the fun."

Ruth smiled. "I think I might need to see some of these things in action."

"Good idea." Gabriel said it as though it had been her idea. Maybe that would help convince her that she wanted to stay longer. "You can wash up first."

She went right to the sink as though making bread was a good idea no matter whose it was. It wasn't long before Gabriel had set Ruth to work pounding the oats while he gathered a bunch of ingredients onto his counter. He had everything ready and was moving things around to disguise how frustrated he was by her lack of progress.

He wanted to grab her hand on the tool and demonstrate the proper technique. He couldn't do that because it looked like the scene in every girly movie where the guy makes an excuse for physical contact.

It wasn't an excuse in this case. She was doing it wrong, and he couldn't show her the right way to pulverize oats because he didn't want to insult her intelligence with such an obvious ploy to get closer. Not when they were just starting to have a relationship again.

"This doesn't seem to be working," Ruth said.

A demonstration, despite being a terrible idea, became even more tempting when Gabriel realized the first words to come to mind were *that's because you're doing it wrong.* A grouchy tone was not entirely conducive to relationship building either.

Ruth glanced over her shoulder at him. "What am I doing wrong?"

He took his eyes off the back of her hand and away from thoughts of touching it. Some tension dissolved. "Well... you're not trying to make friends with the oats, you're trying to crush them."

"So I need to hit them harder?" She lifted the hand holding the pestle to her shoulder and froze. "I'm afraid if I pound them like this I'm going to send them flying out of the bowl."

"You might," he said.

She rolled her eyes at his lack of helpfulness.

"Okay. Keep your hand closer to the bowl. Just apply more pressure and twist and wiggle it against the oats."

Ruth tried to follow his instructions and after a few seconds, she smiled. "They're starting to break up."

"Good. Keep pounding."

Ruth lifted the pestle over her head, threatening to smash the oats and purposefully send them flying. She lowered it to crush them properly as soon as she got a laugh.

Gabriel enjoyed the threat because he knew it was empty. He also loved that she enjoyed it; she was getting comfortable around him again. He mixed some of the other ingredients while she did the fun part. She only used the dough hook for a minute before she complained that her arm was getting tired. They soon had the dough rising, and they watched it. They actually stood in his kitchen watching the dough rise.

They were so busy talking they didn't care how much time was passing. Most of the conversation revolved around old memories. Some of the talk came from college, where they had made memories without each other. They even talked about saints a little.

Ruth stayed long enough to have a slice of the still-warm bread. "Oh, this is good," she said. "Possibly even worth the trouble."

"Possibly?"

She took another bite. "Yeah. It's worth it. Do you think – ?" She bit her lip as she cut herself off.

"Do I think what?" Gabriel asked.

"Well, I was going to ask if you wanted to show me what that grinder does next week. But I..." She just kind of shook her head. It seemed she was warring between being a polite guest and an eager friend.

Gabriel definitely wanted her to come down on the side of friend. "Go ahead and ask me if I want to."

She smiled self-consciously. "I sort of already did."

"No, you said you were going to ask me, but you didn't really ask."

"Fine. Do you want to show me the grinder in action?"

"Yes." He opened the cabinet it was in.

"Next week," Ruth said. "Do you want to show it to me after we work on the church stuff next week?"

He closed the cabinet as though he'd been joking about pulling it out right then. "Sure. Next week we'll plan out some saint talk and then have hamburgers."

"Great." Ruth picked up another slice of bread to take home with her.

The afternoon would have been worth the time for Gabriel even if the bread had failed.

11

Ruth's family teased her when she stayed in a dress after church because they knew she was going to see Gabriel. They teased her again the next week about "letting herself go" when she changed into shorts. She figured that if they were going to give her a hard time no matter what, she might as well be comfortable.

She swapped her pink dress for a pink shirt and gray shorts. There was a fair amount of pink in her wardrobe despite the fact that more than one person had told her it wasn't the most flattering color for a redhead. Ruth stood in front of the mirror in her bedroom. Maybe she was missing something and maybe she was just being stubborn, but she didn't see a problem. She liked pink and she was going to wear it.

A car parked on the street as she walked past it. She stopped to greet Joseph as he got out and waved. Her hands flew to her hips as he got close enough to hear her. "And what was your excuse for missing Friday again?"

He groaned and cast his eyes to the ground.

Ruth waited. She was glad he at least looked guilty. They'd already exchanged a few texts about his latest absence, but she wanted to make him say it out loud.

Joseph held his hands out apologetically. "I forgot."

"You forgot?" Ruth sighed as though she was more

exasperated than she really was. "You forgot it was Friday or you forgot that your favorite sister wanted you to come?"

A faint smile flickered across his face. As the only girl, she got a lot of mileage out of the favorite sister joke. Then he shrugged helplessly. "You know my schedule is always changing. I was enjoying a quiet evening at home when it hit me I was supposed to be somewhere else. But I set a reminder for this Friday. I will be there."

"I'll believe that when I see it," Ruth said. She turned towards the back door to lead her brother into the house.

"By the way, Isaac said you've been doing a good job with the group," Joseph said as he followed. "I wonder what Mom's making for lunch today."

Ruth was happy to talk about food. She was more gratified than she wanted to admit to hear of her big brother's approval. Best not to dwell on that. Lunch was delicious as always. It was peppered with laughs, talk of the future grandchild, and more than one question about how Ruth was getting along with Gabriel. Good was apparently an insufficient answer.

Joseph eventually grabbed a basketball and invited others to join him outside. Ruth was the only one to accept. She had second thoughts as she began to dribble across the driveway. It was sunny and very warm. Visiting Gabe dressed casually was one thing, visiting him smelly and sticky was another. "How about Horse?" she asked. Less running and sweatiness.

"All right." Joseph held his hands up for the ball. "I'll go first."

She tossed it a bit harder than necessary, which made him flinch and smile as he caught it.

Joseph turned and walked out to 3-point range. If he made some far shots, it would be a short game. Ruth didn't have the strength to throw it that far, at least not with any kind of decent aim. Fortunately, he missed his first one.

Ruth chased down the ball then lined herself up for an easy shot. It hit the mark with a satisfying swish.

On Joseph's turn, he stood in place and dribbled slowly before he looked at the basket. "So how many single women, other than you of course, have been coming to your new group?"

"Oh. No beating around the bush, huh?"

Joseph sighed as he copied Ruth's basket. "I can't afford to beat around the bush. I'm twenty-nine, and there aren't a lot of fish in this little town. Especially ones who might be willing to be saddled with all this." He pointed to himself with a self-deprecating smile. His eyes also crinkled as he processed his own mixed metaphor.

"I suppose you are a unique package." She meant it to be teasing. But he was a man who knew what he wanted, and that did sort of limit his choices. Joseph hadn't been to school full time since high school, but he had taken some theology courses while he considered entering a seminary. He'd felt called to have a family first – a large family – then possibly serve the church as a permanent deacon later. He couldn't marry someone who didn't want those same things. "Well," she said, getting back to his question, "Ella Sweet is the only one who's been there more than once. But we are only three meetings in."

Joseph caught a rebound looking thoughtful. It appeared Ella was not out of the question, which could be good news for both of them. Not that Ruth planned to share that news. She'd be happy to see Ella and Joseph get together but had no interest in playing matchmaker with her brother.

Ruth won the first game of Horse. Joseph had just won the

second when Isaac and Jessica came out of the house. "Heading home?" Ruth asked.

"Yeah," Isaac said. "I guess we'll see you on Friday, and we'll see you..." He paused as he pointed to Joseph.

"You'll see him on Friday, too," Ruth said.

"I won't forget."

The four of them smiled with pleasant goodbyes. Isaac and Jessica went to their car. Joseph went inside to say goodbye to his parents. Ruth went inside her tiny little house to get her purse. She needed to stop at Seymour's on her way to Gabe's.

The sign out front actually read Andauk IGA. The town's grocery store had been owned by a family named Seymour for something like fifty years. Though it had now been Andauk IGA for nearly a decade, locals still called it Seymour's. Except for the occasional middle-schooler who dubbed it Iga as though he or she was the first person to pronounce the letters like a word.

Ruth entered the store and went straight to the freezer aisle. Gabriel was supplying everything for the hamburgers but said she could bring dessert. She'd been undecided most of the week. After the basketball that included more running around than she'd intended, ice cream sounded really good. She picked a pint of mint chocolate chip.

The ice cream would melt if she took too long to get to Gabe's apartment. Ruth didn't believe for a second that was why she felt rushed. She was looking forward to seeing him again so much she was all fluttery inside. She held up the ice cream as he opened the door.

"Oh." He smiled and nodded. "Good choice."

"It needs to go in the freezer." *And that's why I look so impatient to come inside.*

Ruth made herself comfortable at his table while he put away the ice cream for later. Several by now familiar books were already stacked up. "I suppose you'll need to return these to the library eventually," she said.

"I just renewed them a second time. And do you remember Julia who was at our first meeting? She works at the library so I mentioned the group. She said she might come again. I should have asked her if there's a limit on the number of times you can renew something."

"Hmm." Ruth considered. "I guess if you get to the limit you can return them, and then I'll check them out for a while."

"True. We could probably take turns indefinitely."

Ruth nodded, pleased with the idea of this partnership stretching out indefinitely.

"I feel like I've been picking all the saints so far," Gabriel said as he joined her at the table. He pushed the stack of books in front of her. "Tell me who you want to discuss this week. Or what topic."

That was going to be difficult. Whenever Ruth looked through the saints in these books, they all sounded interesting. But only a little interesting. She couldn't seem to muster the desire to dig deeper on any of them.

Gabriel leaned back in his chair. "We have a long time before we need to start on dinner."

He'd obviously picked up on her reluctance to name a topic. His patience was unfortunate. She opened one of the books and began to read a random page. Then she turned to another page. It seemed that everyone she read about was born, prayed a lot, then martyred. She was wondering where that wonderful variety was that someone had mentioned at their first meeting. Plus, Ruth was very aware of Gabriel sitting nearby, watching and waiting for her to be inspired with an idea. The pressure wasn't helping.

She kept reading, skipping to more random pages. Then she read one line that flooded her brain with too many thoughts to process. "Oh, wow," she said. "Have you ever heard this? It's about St. Nicholas." She glanced up to make sure she had his attention. As far as she could tell, he'd never stopped paying attention.

"St. Nicholas as in Santa Claus?"

"Yeah. I mean, the same one that inspired Santa Claus."

"Shouldn't we save him for December?" Gabriel asked. "He'd be an obvious choice around Christmas."

"Maybe. We don't have to talk about him specifically, but listen to this. It says the most popular legend about him is that he once brought to life three boys who had been murdered and hidden by a butcher."

"Uh..." Gabriel appeared uncertain as to how to respond. "I thought you didn't want to talk about gruesome things."

"I don't," Ruth said. "But have you heard that story before?"

Gabriel shook his head.

"Me neither. So my first thought was that I thought the coins through the window story was the most popular. You know, how they landed in the stockings that had been hung to dry and relates to the current hanging of stockings?"

"That one I've heard," Gabriel said.

"Right. So maybe the one about giving life to murdered children is the most well-known in other areas or... But that's not really what I want to talk about. The story made me think of several other legends about saints – like Francis and the wolf – and how the stories can still be important even if they are embellished or completely made up because of the moral truth behind them."

Ruth was talking so fast, she hoped she was still making sense. "Like with Nicholas, both those stories show him to be kind and generous. Kindness and generosity are important attributes to promote and model even if he only ever handed over coins and didn't throw them through a window anonymously. So could we try to talk about a bunch of these legends and why the lessons are valid even if some or all of the facts are made up? Do you know what I mean?"

"I do. And I think it's a great idea." His enthusiasm was evident as he began to flip through another book. "I saw something that might work earlier."

Ruth jotted down St. Nicholas and a page number before she turned the page to see what else she could find.

"Here it is," Gabriel said. "His name is Ignatius but not the one from Loyola. He lived in the first century and is said to have never stopped calling the name of Jesus even as wild animals ripped out his throat in the Colosseum."

"Well... it's obvious that relates to the importance of turning to God in times of trouble. But it goes back into gross territory."

Gabriel turned the page. "That's what I thought you'd say."

"Write it down anyway," Ruth said. "We'll put it at the bottom of our list just in case we can't find enough less gross ones."

Gabriel made note of the page number.

It began to look unlikely that they'd need it as they found and listed many legends. Gabriel searched through some websites while Ruth continued through the books. They wrote down all the stories and talked about what morals or attributes they illustrated while they decided which would be most interesting to discuss on Friday.

The time passed so quickly that it was soon a half hour past when they'd planned to eat, and they hadn't even started making dinner.

"Wow, look at the time," Gabriel said. "I'm sure we have enough to fill an hour and a half."

"I think we might have enough to fill two hours and a half. Or I mean, two meetings. Assuming the others like the topic, maybe we could save anyone we don't get to for a future week when we don't have any other ideas. Instead of doing legends two weeks in a row."

"Yeah, a back-up topic will be good." Gabriel was clearing away their books and notes. "Are you hungry?"

"A little." That was the honest answer since she tended to eat a big lunch when her mom was cooking.

Gabriel had already moved to the kitchen counter.

Ruth watched him spread out all the pieces of the meat grinder.

"There you go," he said.

"What do you mean?"

"Don't you want to see if you can put it together?"

Ruth didn't know if he was kidding. On the one hand, she was expecting to stand back and stay out of his way. He'd seemed anxious about letting her use some of his other kitchen tools. On the other hand, looking at the pieces did make her curious if she could figure it out.

Before she could respond, Gabe said, "*I'd* like to see if you can put it together."

It wasn't a challenge. He said it as though letting her try would be fun for both of them.

Ruth stepped up to the challenge that wasn't a challenge. Her fingers stopped just before making contact with the first piece. "Wait. This thing grinds up meat," she said. "I'm not going to hurt myself with it, am I?"

"No," he said. Then his lips pinched together thoughtfully. "Well, I think you'd have to be trying to hurt yourself. I'm sure you'll be fine as long as you handle the pieces carefully."

Ruth picked up a spiral of metal, perhaps too cautiously. It immediately slipped out of her grasp and clinked against more metal. She turned sheepishly towards Gabriel. "Maybe we should be worried about whether or not this thing is safe from me."

This time he laughed. "It's metal. I don't think you could break it even if you were trying to break it."

"All right." Unable to come up with any more concerns, Ruth plunged ahead with fitting the pieces together. It didn't take her very long, though there was some trial and error. She could tell where all the parts went, but the order to get them there was important and less obvious.

Gabriel ground up the meat. They both preferred that Ruth watch that step. And the step that involved touching raw meat with bare hands. The hamburgers, eventually, tasted delicious. Ruth could not attribute the flavor to appreciation for a bygone era as Gabriel might. She was too fond of the current moment to desire any other.

12

Mr. Sweet was standing inside the door when Ruth arrived Monday morning. "You're here!" he exclaimed.

"I'm here," she said, speaking as much about her arrival to a familiar scene as her arrival at work.

"Please come make my printer behave," Mr. Sweet said.

"Have you checked for a paper jam?"

"Why would I check for a paper jam?"

"Because it's been the problem most of the time."

"I meant why would *I* check for a paper jam?" He tapped his chest. "When I have a self-proclaimed printer-fixing expert." He pointed at Ruth with an ingratiating smile.

"I have never called myself that," she said.

"Called yourself what?"

"A printer-fixing expert."

"Maybe you just did."

Ruth closed her eyes. It was as though she was having a conversation with one of her brothers and not her boss. "Do you want me to look at the printer?"

He turned towards his office and waved both arms to usher her inside.

Ella sat at her desk wearing a smile that said she was paying more attention to the exchange next to her than the open file in front of her. Ruth went into Mr. Sweet's office and pulled a wrinkled piece of paper from the back of his printer. She talked through what she was doing for her boss's benefit. He appeared to be listening. Then again, he appeared to be listening just as closely as the last five times she'd explained it.

She crumpled the already ruined paper into a ball and tossed it at Mr. Sweet.

"Thank you," he said as he caught it.

"You're welcome." As she walked out of his office, she felt that paper ball hit her in the middle of her back.

Ella cracked up.

Ruth picked up the paper with an amused sigh. She would not have guessed when she started that working for an insurance agent could be fun. She also didn't know that Ella would become such a good friend, the kind of friend Ruth could talk to about anything.

And for better or worse, Ella was the kind of friend who could ask her about anything. "Are you dating Gabriel yet?" she asked.

"What? No." Ruth answered quickly, ready to chastise Ella for the teasing.

But Ella looked confused by the answer, which confused Ruth. The two women made questioning faces at each other until Ella said, "But I thought you said you were having dinner with him last night?"

"I did. But it wasn't anything.... romantic. We were just hanging out a little after we finished planning. And by the way, we're going to have an awesome discussion on Friday."

"No changing the subject," Ella said. "You and Gabriel spent some extra time together last week, too. Why isn't this leading anywhere?"

"Because you have no patience," Ruth said. The door behind her clicked closed as Mr. Sweet shut himself in his office. Whether this was because he thought the girls could use some privacy or because he had work to do didn't matter to Ruth since it gave them privacy either way.

Ella sighed. "I think you have too much patience."

"Patience is a virtue," Ruth countered. "How can I have too much of it?"

"When you use it to cover your fear."

That hurt. No one liked to be called a chicken.

Ella offered an apologetic smile. "Sorry. You two are getting along well though and you have a history that suggests you'd be good together. I'm just suggesting you go ahead and ask him if he'd... like to do something that is romantic."

"Maybe I am a little scared," Ruth said. "This church thing is giving us a great excuse to spend time together. But if I admit I'd like us to spend more time and he doesn't... the excuse will go from a blessing to a curse."

"I grant you that would be awkward." Ella shifted some papers and glanced at the clock. "But I don't think he'd turn you down. Why would he have gotten upset about the thing with Eric if he wasn't interested in you?"

"That might have been a good point. Four years ago." Ruth was ready to move on. "I gave Joseph a hard time about forgetting. He's going to be there this Friday for sure."

Ella opened her mouth, paused, then said, "I think we should have pizza for this week's splurge day."

"I thought we weren't allowed to change the subject."

"You're not," Ella said playfully. "I have seniority here, so I'm allowed to change the subject."

"That's a perk of seniority?" Ruth snorted. "I'll have to bring that up at the next staff meeting."

Ella laughed, but she spoke seriously through it. "Please don't mention staff meetings to my dad. He would totally have the three of us getting together to vote on stupid things like what brand of pens to buy."

****

"So we're agreed on Burger Brothers?" Ella smiled hopefully. She'd been talking about pizza all week and now that it was Friday her tune had changed.

"We had burgers last week," Ruth said.

"But I had pizza last night."

"That's not my fault."

Ella's mom had served a wonderful homemade pizza Thursday night, which was the cause of Ella's new request. Ruth honestly didn't mind switching to burgers. She only wanted to watch Ella squirm as she justified the switch. "I know," Ella said. "It's probably my fault. I must've somehow put pizza in my mom's head this week. And you will be so kind to agree to wait a week after I've talked it up. Please."

"Okay." Ruth didn't need much squirming. "Do you want to pick them up or should I?"

"Let's both go." Ella stood up as she spoke. She stepped towards her dad's office before she realized he was already in the doorway.

He leaned against the frame, arms crossed, ankles crossed, mock glowering eyes. "Going somewhere?" he asked.

"Do you mind if Ruth and I head to Burger Brothers for lunch?"

"Do I mind?" He repeated the question as though he just really didn't know how to answer it.

Ella flopped back into her chair as she turned to Ruth. "I guess we'll have to stay here until someone decides to give us permission."

"I guess so," Ruth said.

"I sure hope we don't die of starvation."

"Little chance of that," Mr. Sweet said, amused by the dramatics. "You two get out of here and enjoy your lunch." He pushed himself away from the door.

"Thanks, Dad," Ella said as they left.

Ruth waved her appreciation.

Burger Brothers had a red and white striped awning that called attention from clear down the street. The sign above it had a cartoonish man grinning inside each of the Bs. When either of the brothers who owned the place – Chip and Chuck – were asked which goofy cartoon he was, his answer was, "The handsomer one."

It appeared that Chip was in charge that day because his wife zipped by on her neon green roller skates as Ruth and Ella entered. Paula was an apple-shaped woman of around fifty who looked ridiculous on skates. Ridiculous and welcoming. She circled back with a bright smile under her mop of curly blond and gray hair. "Afternoon, ladies," she said.

Ruth returned the smile. "Hello, Paula."

"Make sure you have your orders ready, ladies. Chip is feeling a little well done today." Paula delivered the friendly warning, then dashed towards the kitchen.

Ruth turned to Ella, whose expression mirrored her own bewilderment. They shrugged at each other. They always got the same thing so there wasn't much to have ready regardless.

There were two people in front of them in line. The woman who raised Jack Russel terriers was already taking her receipt. A man in a police uniform stepped up to order. He'd been a local football hero before he became a public servant.

"I'll have a veggie burger and a large Coke, please," he said.

Chip expelled so much air that his shoulders sagged. It was as though he was deflating. "It's not a burger if it doesn't have meat," he said. "It's a veggie patty."

"Okay, I would love to have your veggie *patty* then."

Chip stared at him for a moment, looking like someone waiting for an apology. Then he said, "Would you like me to burn some flavor into it?"

"The usual," Mr. Policeman answered with a nod.

A strange, plastered-on smile bloomed across Chip's face and stayed there while he finished the transaction. It disappeared when he saw Ruth and Ella. "Must be Friday," he said, instead of a greeting.

"Yeah, we're back," Ruth said. "We'd like two standard cheeseburgers, please."

Chip had a mustache and eyebrows that were nearly as thick. He raised one of them. "That's it?"

"Yes." She and Ella never ordered drinks because they took the food back to the office where they had water waiting. They didn't need fries, but Ruth considered some under the weight of the accusing gaze.

Chip gave another deep sigh. "I mean, you don't want me to add anything or leave something off or otherwise improve my specialty?"

Ruth shook her head earnestly. "No improvements needed."

A tiny smile flashed and Ruth kicked herself for taking his bluster seriously. The man was always difficult. She didn't know why she'd expected today to be different.

He held out his hand for payment.

Ella spoke up as she pulled out a debit card. "It's my turn."

"You want these to go, right?" Chip asked. He didn't wait for an answer. "I'll have someone wrap them up."

Paula popped through the door from the kitchen just then. She did a terribly ungraceful pirouette on her skates before she went right back through the doors.

Ruth and Ella stood to the side to wait for their lunch. They could hear Chip calling out instructions. He took orders through a window and only had to turn around to be in the kitchen. When their burgers were ready, Paula stacked the wrapped burgers on one hand and held them through the window.

Ruth was closer so she grabbed both of them. "Thank you," she said.

"See you again next Friday." Paula waved as she rolled away.

There was no point in Ruth trying to catch her to explain they were having pizza next Friday. They'd be back soon enough.

13

No one was standing outside the school when Ruth pulled into the parking lot. She figured Gabriel was already inside. Not that she was late. She simply expected him to be earlier.

Ella hugged herself for warmth as they hurried to the building. September weather could be crazy. Sunday it had been too hot for Ruth to play basketball. Friday she needed to keep her jacket zipped.

The sounds of moving furniture echoed through the empty hall. The tables were already moved and the chairs in a circle when Ruth and Ella entered the room. Gabriel had help though. Sebastian smiled tentatively and gestured to the two closest chairs.

"Hello," Ruth said, trying to include both the guys in her greeting as she accepted one of the offered chairs. She was getting used to Sebastian, or she guessed that was why she no longer tensed up at the sight of him.

Ella sat next to her and addressed Gabriel. "Ruth won't tell me what we're going to talk about, but she said it's good this week."

"Of course she said it's good," Gabriel said. "It was her idea."

Isaac walked in just in time to continue the teasing. "Ruth had an idea?" He sounded shocked. Jessica was with him this week, which distracted everyone.

"Jessica," Ruth said, "glad you made it. Are you feeling okay today?"

Sebastian eyed her pregnant belly as she sat near him. "You been having a lot of morning sickness?"

"No," Jessica said. "No, in fact, I don't think I've felt anything that would qualify as morning sickness. I'm just exhausted all the time." She spontaneously yawned right as she finished talking, which caused a few sympathetic chuckles.

Joseph was the last to arrive. He was applauded for showing up. Ruth and Isaac started clapping and the others quickly joined in.

He sat down with a disapproving expression. "Come on, guys. Was that really necessary?"

"It was totally necessary," Ruth assured him.

He smiled as he rolled his eyes at her. Then he said hello to everyone else around the room.

"Okay, I guess it's time to get started." Ruth tried to make herself sound serious.

Gabriel led a prayer. That sobered them up for about the length of one Our Father.

Then Isaac said, "St. Ruth, right? Your big idea is to talk about how you compare to St. Ruth."

Ruth chose to ignore the comment, as well as the snicker from Ella. "We're going to talk about legends today," she said. "We thought it'd be interesting to try to identify lessons in some of the more, um, wild stories about the saints."

She looked around the room. She saw a lot of curiosity but also some puzzled expressions. "So here's an easy example." She opened her notes to make sure she attributed the story to the right saint. "St. Martin of Tours. It's said that one very cold night in the fourth century, he encountered a nearly naked and freezing beggar on the street. Martin used his sword to cut his cloak in half and gave half of it to the beggar. Soon afterward, he received a vision. He saw Christ wearing half his cloak. Now," she paused for a breath, "the lesson here is rather obvious. Jesus said himself that what we do for others, we do for him. Even if Martin never saw a vision, the story can still remind us of that important truth."

"Yeah." Isaac nodded.

"The first part doesn't have to be entirely true either," Sebastian said.

"The first part?" Gabriel and Ruth asked about his meaning at the same time.

"Well, even if Martin was a wealthy man who gave a spare cloak, but people thought it was more dramatic to say he cut his in half, it's still someone giving to someone in need."

"True." Gabriel looked at Ruth for another example.

She checked her notes. The setting made her weirdly nervous considering that most of the people in the room were family or close friends. "We did say we'd start with an easy one. Let's see if we can identify the lesson in the legend of Wilgefortis. This one was classified as most likely a myth. Wilgefortis – and I'm probably saying that wrong – was a young woman who wanted to join a convent. Her father, a pagan, promised her in marriage against her wishes. She prayed for help. God gave her a beard, which made her suitor withdraw his offer. Her father was so angry the marriage didn't happen that he had her crucified."

The others were staring at Ruth when she finished. She and Gabriel hadn't figured out a moral reason to pass on that particular story. She shrugged at them. "What do you guys think?"

"Um, be careful what you wish for?" Jessica suggested.

A few moments of silence followed because no one could think of a better possibility.

Then Ella fidgeted next to Ruth. It seemed she was working up the courage to speak into the void. "Well... I guess I have to point out that... as much as I wouldn't want a beard, it'd be better than being forced to marry someone I didn't want to marry."

"But then she was crucified," Gabriel pointed out.

"Yeah, even that..." Ella looked uncertainly around the room. "A lifetime of slavery, which is essentially what a forced marriage at the time amounted to, or a relatively quick death?"

A few people nodded.

"So you're saying," Sebastian said, "that the message here might be like God works in mysterious ways?"

Ella sort of shrugged and nodded.

"Yes," Isaac said. "Maybe. I could see the story being passed on to remind us that God doesn't always answer prayers the way we expect."

"Right." Joseph was coming on board with the concept. "Even something that seems bad, like a woman growing a beard, God can use that for good."

"I think we cracked it," Gabriel said.

Agreement flew around the room, along with a few high fives.

Gabriel nudged Ruth's arm as Isaac said, "Give us another one."

"Okay. Here's another one that's presumed to be fiction but still potentially instructive. St. Brendon the Navigator is an Irish saint. He was a monk. The story is that he and some fellow monks were at sea, some sort of long voyage, and they landed on the back of a whale and thought it was an island. It was Easter so they got out of the boat to celebrate a Mass. But when they lit a fire to prepare a feast after, it woke up the whale, and they had to scramble back into the boat to escape."

"I can see why that story would be popular," Sebastian said. "It's an interesting story even without any deep meaning."

Jessica tilted her head skeptically. "They thought a whale was an island?"

"Well," Ruth said, "it sounds far-fetched, but I have never personally been on the back of a whale or a small island in the middle of an ocean."

"I suppose if you'd been at sea long enough..." Joseph put a hand on his stomach. "Especially if you were at all queasy, you might not bother to question anything solid."

There were a few sea-sickness jokes and comments on the whale's thoughts before Gabriel challenged them to find a spiritual meaning in the story.

"There was an Easter Mass," Sebastian said.

"Right." Joseph nodded thoughtfully. "Perhaps this is a God will provide message. They needed a place to celebrate Easter and the whale happened to nap right in front of them. But –" He held up a finger as a lightbulb came on. "They didn't get to have the feast so maybe it's about priorities."

"Exactly." Isaac emphatically agreed with his brother. "God provides for needs but not necessarily wants. They got in their worship time but not their party time. This is clearly a story about remembering what's important."

"Clearly," Ruth said dryly. Though she was thinking again that her brothers were pretty smart.

"The only possible explanation," Isaac said with a grin.

"Let's try another," Ella said.

Ruth checked her list to see who was next. "Sebald is associated with many miracles from the eighth century. One is the miracle of the icicles. It's said that he took refuge with a peasant family during a snowstorm. They were out of fuel and the fire was dying. He told the woman to put icicles on the embers. When she did, it gave off enough heat to keep everyone warm."

"Oh, I got this one," Joseph said.

All eyes in the room landed on him. After a dramatic pause, he said, "Blessings can come from unexpected sources."

Ruth was surprised into silence because she'd expected a joke. She guessed that was why no one else responded right away either, though she wasn't entirely sure why they all thought he would try to be funny.

Finally, Isaac said, "I think he nailed it."

Everyone began to nod and then look at Ruth. She took it as her cue to toss out another. She was starting to feel a little like a game show host. "Well, this one isn't really a story. I just wrote it down because it reminded me of my mom. St. Polycarp lived around the end of the first century –"

"Mom's not that old," Joseph said.

She smiled – now he was in the mood to joke – and continued. "There's a report that he once said he'd rather go deaf than have to listen to and argue with any more heretics. When I first read that, I thought about what my mom always said about listening to garbage and..."

She trailed off because both of her brothers had started nodding knowingly. Together they tapped their ears and then their mouths and said, "Garbage in, garbage out."

Jessica understood and Ruth had explained it to Gabriel. Sebastian gave Ella a sympathetic look as they were the only ones left out.

"It's what our mom used to say, and sometimes still says," Ruth explained. "Mostly when we were teenagers and wanted to watch a movie or listen to a song with a lot of foul language."

"We'd insist we knew better than to repeat it," Joseph said.

"And Mom would argue that too much would desensitize us and eventually..." He tapped his ear and mouth again. "Garbage in, garbage out."

"I think I'm old enough to admit there's some truth to that."

Jessica nodded at her husband and put a hand on her belly. "Especially now that we're starting to consider what to teach our own kids."

"But I don't think that's what Polycarp was talking about," Isaac said.

"Listening to heresies can be a lot more dangerous than a few bad words," Joseph agreed.

"Also, there was that part about arguing," Sebastian pointed out. "Do you think he'd want to avoid that simply because it'd be exhausting or because of the weight of the responsibility of passing on truth?"

Gabriel shook his head. "Well, we can't ask him, but I'd think both those reasons would be valid."

"Okay, sorry for bringing it up." Ruth wanted to keep the meeting lighter. "I'm not sure why that even made me think of Mom, but let's get back to the legends. Here's one about..."

"What about Patrick?" Sebastian asked.

"Patrick?" Ruth hadn't found who was next yet so she felt more intrigued than interrupted.

Sebastian sounded apologetic though. "I'm sorry. You were talking. I just wondered if Patrick was on your list."

Ruth shook her head.

"The one about the snakes?" Isaac asked.

"Yeah." Sebastian hesitated for a moment, then said, "The saint legend I'm most familiar with is Patrick driving all the snakes out of Ireland."

"Oh, I think I have heard that," Gabriel said.

"I have a theory on that." Joseph stopped and waved his hands as though to rewind his words. "I mean, it's not my theory. We talked about that in one of my classes. A lot of these stories and traditions were passed on orally before literacy was widespread. And some artists showed snakes to represent the devil because of the serpent in the Garden of Eden. So as Patrick was spreading Christianity, he might have been causing some demons to retreat. It could be that pictures of those metaphorical snakes were interpreted literally at some point."

"That makes sense," Sebastian said.

There was a pause while everyone let the idea sink in. Then Ruth felt it was her turn to talk again. "Here's a guy who is said to have literally moved a mountain." His story brought more laughs and serious points to the group. Ruth still had several on her list when the time ran out and people were reluctant to leave. They had to rush to get the room back in order just as Mrs. Donnelly arrived to lock up.

Ella walked down the hall with Gabriel and Ruth while the others went ahead. "That was fun," she said.

"I think it was our best one yet," Gabriel agreed.

Ruth nodded along with both of them. She had enjoyed it despite nagging worries about the low turnout.

Joseph was waiting by the outside door when they caught up. "What do you think?" he asked Ella. "Should we keep these two as leaders?"

"I think so," she answered with a shy smile.

Ruth tipped her head to get Gabriel to step to the side with her. Just because she wasn't playing matchmaker didn't mean she wouldn't stay out of the way. "Sunday at three?" she asked him.

It looked as though Gabriel was going to say one thing and stopped himself. "That sounds good," was what he said instead.

"And we'll do dinner after?"

"Yes." Ruth held out the word, trying to decide if she wanted to ask what his first thought had been. He seemed genuinely happy with the idea of getting together so maybe it didn't matter. "You did say you were going to let me try out the masher."

"I guess we're going to need something to mash." His eyes went towards the sky for a moment. "Bananas?"

"Bananas?" Ruth repeated.

"For banana bread. Yeah, that would need oat flour, too. We'll have lots of fun with that."

She smiled at how animated his old kitchen gadgets made him. "That does sound... fun."

"Why did you hesitate?" His eagerness was quickly replaced with concern. "Do you not like banana bread? I thought you liked bananas."

"Oh, I do. I just wondered what we'd have with it."

"I'll figure something out," Gabriel said. He held up his hand at the same time to acknowledge that Joseph was leaving.

"Later, guys," he said.

Ruth told Gabriel she'd see him on Sunday and returned to Ella's side. She gave Ruth an expectant look.

"What?"

"Don't act all innocent," Ella said. "You and Gabriel were just making plans, weren't you?"

"The same plans we've had the last several weeks. Coming up with questions for the group."

Ella seemed to let it go as they got into the car. After a moment she said, "Look, I'm sorry if I'm being pushy. I'm just excited about you two maybe getting together."

"It's okay," Ruth said. And it was. She was excited as well and happy Ella kept bringing it up so she had an excuse to talk about Gabe. "I have actually been thinking about what you said."

"About you asking him out?"

"Yeah."

Ella smiled broadly. "And you're gonna do it?"

"Not yet."

The corners of her mouth dropped.

"I think right now I need to just be grateful that we have any kind of relationship again," Ruth said. "But I will say something if... I'm going to be brave and look for signs that the time is right. Then I'll say something."

14

Ruth had told Ella that she'd thought about asking Gabe out. That was true. It was also a huge understatement. The thought was on her mind constantly. It snuck up on her when she was brushing her teeth, an image of another brush next to hers someday. It drifted to the background when she was working or talking to someone else. Even in the background it was still present. And when she pushed her car door closed and stood facing his increasingly familiar apartment, the thought jumped out and nearly tackled her.

How would she recognize the right moment? Working side by side in Gabe's kitchen had provided a lot of really nice moments. They made a great team, at times comfortable, fun, calm, serious. Whether they were laughing over eggshells in the batter or disagreeing about a question for the next Friday, they got through it together and closer than before. It was more and more like old times and yet not quite the same.

Ruth was truly grateful to have her old friend back in her life. But she wanted more. She did not want to get stuck sharing moments here and there when she could see the potential of sharing a whole life with Gabriel. Already they were stuck in this Sunday only rhythm that hinted they might stop seeing each other all together if their young adult group ended.

It seemed simple enough to overcome the limitation. Do you

want to take a walk with me sometime? How about we meet for lunch? This movie sounds interesting. Care to see it with me? All easy questions in Ruth's head, but Ruth had spent weeks wondering if she was brave enough to ask any of them. She and Gabriel weren't teenagers anymore. If she asked him to do something outside the current planning, it would be a date. And she'd be admitting she wanted it to be a date.

The question itself wasn't the real problem though. The courage Ruth needed was to clear the way to asking. She felt that they needed to talk about the past first. It had almost come up a few times. They had talked about college and finding jobs, things that they'd done apart. They had also talked about plenty of things they'd done together. Whenever the conversation drifted towards the split, it was quickly steered away. Neither wanted to talk about what happened between them. The knowledge was still there, the knowledge that they'd both given up on their relationship once before. Ruth needed Gabriel to know she wouldn't do it again before she asked him to move forward with her.

She walked up his sidewalk clutching a cast iron trivet. The apartment had two units on the front and two on the back. The door next to Gabriel's popped open, and a thoroughly disheveled man of about sixty exited. He was wearing four or five shirts of different styles and sizes. The top layer was unbuttoned flannel. Somewhere in the middle was something with a collar that was sticking up on one side. His cuffs hung loose over longer sleeves and there was a large tear under one knee of his jeans.

He visibly startled when he saw Ruth. Then he smiled timidly and gave an exaggerated bow in her direction.

She stopped and said, "Hello, um, good afternoon." People called the man Jojo, but she didn't know if that was his real name.

Even if it was, it seemed too familiar to address someone she'd never spoken to directly before.

Jojo pointed at the trivet she held with a question in his eyes.

"It's a trivet," she said.

He mimed touching something hot and then stuck his finger in his mouth.

Ruth didn't understand. Jojo was a town mystery. No one ever heard him speak. Some people said he couldn't. Some said he chose not to. The reasons given were imaginative at best and insulting at worst.

Jojo stepped closer. Though he and his clothes looked clean, a strong odor came with him.

Ruth tried not to react to the stench.

He pretended to touch something hot again and then pointed at the trivet.

"Oh, yes, it protects the table from hot pans."

He smiled, either because he was glad to be right or because she understood his question. Maybe both. Then he pointed at Gabriel's door with his eyes wide.

"It's for Gabriel," she said with a nod. "Not really a present, but... he likes old things."

Jojo pointed at himself and ruffled his shaggy gray hair.

Ruth wasn't sure if he was saying he also liked old things or that he was an old thing. She tried to smile politely.

His face fell. He tipped an imaginary hat at her and walked briskly past.

After inhaling a bit of fresh air, Ruth felt unsettled by the abrupt departure. She hoped she hadn't offended him. She shrugged it off for the moment and knocked on Gabe's door.

He opened it looking pleased to see her. With his glasses and skinny tie, he could have been cast in a movie from the 1960s, but the nervous twinge in her stomach was far more old-fashioned.

****

Gabriel took in the sight of Ruth standing on his doorstep. The woman of his dreams had come for a visit. It had happened every Sunday for five or six weeks and yet he still felt a little surprised by it. And this time she was holding an awesomely twisted piece of metal. "Hey, where'd you get that?" he asked.

She laughed. "Hello to you, too."

He stepped back to let her inside while he kicked himself for sounding more excited about the trivet than the person holding it. "Glad you made it," he said, which probably implied he had doubts about her word or her ability to drive half a mile. Maybe it was better to focus on the metal because thinking about Ruth scrambled his brain. "What's the story on that?" He held out a hand to ask for a closer look.

"It's my grandma's. Or it was." Ruth was holding it with her fingers wrapped through the metal coils. She dislodged them to place it in Gabriel's hand. "I was over there a few days ago, and I happened to mention how you had a bunch of vintage kitchen items. She said that was her mom's so she couldn't throw it away, but she never uses it and would love to give it to someone who would actually use it."

Gabriel's eyes followed the swirls of metal while she spoke, but his attention latched onto the part of the explanation where she said she was talking about him. Had she just casually mentioned the old friend who'd developed an affinity for weird stuff? Or had she found excuses to talk about the guy she'd been spending a lot of time with? And how she'd like to spend more time with him?

It was nice to think of her telling someone that because

Gabriel wasn't getting any clues himself. Every Sunday she came over and seemed content but didn't give any indication that she'd be okay with more.

Of course, next time she talked to her grandmother she'd be telling her about his overreaction to the old trivet. He'd been absently staring at it, and when he glanced up she was biting her lip to try not to laugh at him. "Well, tell her thanks for me," he said, waving it towards their usual work spot. "Let's get started."

She took a few steps closer to the table. "I didn't know Jojo lived next door to you."

"He does?" Gabriel had never seen anyone and thought the unit might be empty.

"I guess you didn't know that either," she said.

"Guess not." He pulled a book from the stack. "I got a new saint book."

She took it as she sat down and began to page through it. "You haven't already decided who we should study?"

"I had one thought, but it was yours."

"You had my thought?" Ruth smiled teasingly. "I had one good thought, and you stole it? No wonder I'm not contributing much to this partnership."

Gabriel was amused by her playful accusation but not the part she might actually believe. "First of all, you contribute plenty. Second, I didn't steal your thought. I remembered it. There's a page on St. Christopher in there, and it reminded me that back when we were looking for legends you said we should wait on his because we could get a whole meeting out of him."

"I remember saying that, but I'm not sure I remember the reasoning." She turned the pages faster, presumably looking for St. Christopher.

"Page 59," he said.

Her green eyes lifted from the book just long enough to acknowledge his help. She had such pretty eyes, especially with that hint of admiration. For a moment, Gabriel felt like a hero just for remembering a page number.

Ruth found the page and began to read. She put one hand under her chin and her hair dropped over her shoulder. Her eyelids fluttered as she scanned the information. Her lips moved, not with the words but in reaction to them. The bottom one slowly tucked itself between her teeth.

"A couple of thoughts are coming back to me," she said, "but I'm going to need some help to… What?" She stopped talking as she looked up from the book.

"Which thoughts are coming back?" he asked.

She stared for a moment as her eyes narrowed. "You were looking at me funny."

Of course he was looking at her. She was very nice to look at so he couldn't help that. If he happened to look funny at the same time, he probably couldn't help that either. "I'm… sorry?"

She sighed softly. Her eyes darted to the table and back up. "*Why* were you looking at me funny?"

"I… don't know what you mean." He really didn't. He was fairly certain he'd been looking at her the same way for a long time. Today wasn't different.

"Gabe… do you…" She tipped her head back and forth, struggling for words. "Do you, um… do you want to make the cookies first?"

That was clearly two different thoughts mashed together. She closed the book and turned away. It seemed like a bad idea to push for the first thought. And if it had to do with whatever stupid expression on his face started it, he wasn't sure he wanted to know.

"Okay," he said.

They moved away from the table and the homework to find some cookie ingredients. Gabriel's mom was part of a Monday morning bible study, and it was her turn to bring a snack. Gabriel volunteered to make some cookies for her. She'd made a big deal about how generous his offer was even though he knew that she knew it was an excuse to use his cookie press. And she probably knew he was going to enjoy getting Ruth to help him, too. His offer was about as generous as giving someone a ride in a new sports car.

"This one?" Ruth had taken a bowl out of his cabinet.

"Yeah. And a…" He was pointing, about to ask her to grab a spoon as well, but she'd already opened the right drawer. He smiled to think that she knew where he kept things.

They had the dough mixed up in a matter of minutes. Then he showed her how to get the dough into the press.

"I think they make these battery-powered now," Ruth said.

"This is better."

"Because it was first?"

"No," he said. "I mean, yes, the trigger version is the older model, but that's not why I like it in this case. I just prefer not to have to change batteries."

"Oh. The practical side wins out." Ruth smiled as she said it but didn't look at him. She was spreading the metal plates on the counter like she was dealing cards. "A Christmas tree!"

"It's barely October," he said. "We're not making Christmas trees."

"I didn't say we should." She slid it to the side and pointed to another. "This one's interesting."

"I call that the anvil."

"It's not…" She squinted at it as though trying to see what he saw. "It's too… symmetrical to be an anvil. I think most of these are just designs and not supposed to be anything in particular. Like these wavy lines."

"That one is bananas."

"Bananas?"

"Yes."

She shook her head. "No, it isn't. It's just... lines, curvy lines –"

"That look like a bunch of bananas," Gabriel finished.

"Other than the Christmas tree, these two flowers are the only ones that are real shapes."

"Only this one's a flower. That one's an X."

"They're both flowers," she insisted. "Just different kinds of flowers."

"Have you ever seen a flower with only four petals?"

Her face said she had not but wasn't going to admit it. "It's still a flower. Xs are not so fat and rounded."

"Depends on the font."

"This is clearly –" She was suddenly laughing too hard to finish the sentence.

"What's so funny?"

She waved her hand between them as the laugh subsided. "Us. We're totally arguing over the shapes of cookies we haven't made like it matters. It struck me as ridiculous."

"We're not arguing," Gabriel said. Arguing was negative. He was having a great time. "We're just discussing it."

The plate they were discussing clicked against the counter as she put it back down. Her amusement disappeared as quickly as it had come. "I wonder if... there's something we *should* be discussing."

The more serious tone got his attention, the way the words "we need to talk" usually got someone's attention. He braced himself for what she had to say.

Ruth turned her eyes to him. She swallowed nervously. "We, um, haven't talked about..." Her eyes looked past him to the table. "We haven't talked about St. Christopher yet so we should get to work on these cookies so we'll have time."

He nodded, feeling a strange mix of relief and disappointment, then glanced at the books they'd abandoned. When he looked back, Ruth's eyes collided with his. They bounced to the side and back, down and back, down and back again. She nibbled uncertainly on her lip.

The kitchen was filling with heat, and they hadn't turned on the oven yet. Ruth said they should focus on the cookies, but she didn't move a muscle to do so. Gabriel realized that he was seeing Ruth's eyes flickering only out of his peripheral vision. His own eyes were locked on her mouth. He had to be telegraphing a longing, and she wasn't moving. The moment crackled with possibilities.

"Focus." It snapped as Ruth pointed to the metal plates that weren't nearly as entertaining as they were a minute ago. "Let's start with the anvil," she said with a slight eye roll at the name.

"Okay." Gabriel tried to focus. He put the anvil plate on the end and squeezed out the first pan of cookies.

Ruth switched on the oven before she took a turn pressing out a different shape. The silence was becoming uncomfortable. She had to know he'd been about to kiss her. Did she stop him because she didn't want him to or because she didn't want him to *yet?* He'd wait a really long time if she'd only give him permission to add that one word.

"So... speaking of Friday..." Ruth started slowly, aware that they hadn't exactly been speaking of Fridays. Or anything else. "Where has Eric been? I thought he was joining."

Eric. Was he still the problem? Gabriel had a swiftly growing urge to punch something. "I don't know," he said.

Ruth flinched at his dismissive tone, which he immediately regretted. He tried to rein in the mounting frustration. "I mean, he hasn't said anything." He sighed. He didn't want to say what he was about to say. "Maybe you need to ask him."

"I don't see how that would make a difference," she said.

The woman seemed to have no idea the lengths a guy might go to in order to please her, and quite frankly, he wasn't in the mood to point it out. "What about *your* brother?" he asked, hoping to change the subject.

"Which one?"

"Adam. He only came to the first meeting." There. Now they could pretend they were talking about their responsibility to the church and not the fact that Ruth wanted to see his brother. More than him.

"I don't think..." Ruth put down the cookie press and leaned against the counter. "I've actually only seen Adam once since that meeting. He hasn't been coming to our family get-togethers either."

"Oh." Gabriel could tell that bothered Ruth. He put aside his own issues. "Was there a... falling out or something?"

"No, not really. I think he'd just rather be with Kayla."

"You don't like her?"

"No, it's not..." Ruth huffed and closed her eyes. They fixed earnestly on his when she opened them. "Please don't tell anyone I said this, but I really don't like her. I mean, I've tried to be nice anyway and not be obvious about it, but we just don't seem to have anything in common. Sometimes I wonder if she and Adam have that much in common."

"What do you mean?"

"He seems… different. I don't know though. We didn't really spend that much time together when I was in college. That's when he started dating Kayla so he might have changed first, and that's why he…" She put her hands up and down like scales. "Chicken or the egg, right?"

"I think I know what you mean. What's different though?"

"Well, I know he's drifting from the church, which is why I haven't pushed Fridays on him. I know he's not going every Sunday. That's probably why he's not coming to our parents' house. Because he's afraid they'll give him a hard time about it. What bugs me most though is the mean-spirited humor. He and Kayla talk about people they know. They say things like they're joking, but it doesn't even make them laugh. Adam wasn't like that before."

Gabriel nodded his understanding. He had cookie dough residue on his hands. He was aware of it because Ruth seemed to need a hug. He'd moved closer, but he couldn't do anything with his messy hands.

"It's really not my business." Ruth shook off whatever memories she was describing. "But, in general, when you're dating someone… when you think you might marry someone… shouldn't that person bring out your better qualities? Shouldn't you help each other be better?"

"Yes," he said. He wanted to say yes to all of her questions no matter what they were because she was looking at him like she wanted him to say yes.

She smiled at the agreement.

He still couldn't touch her with his greasy hands. But there was nothing on his lips. Nothing on hers. Nothing but space between them. Space that was slowly shrinking.

The timer on the oven beeped. Gabriel would have happily

ignored it, but Ruth quickly washed her hands to pull the pans from the oven. She set the pot holders down and turned to him with a determined expression. "Gabe?"

"Yeah?"

"Can we..." She nervously pushed the pot holders farther back. "It feels like... like we're right back where we were four or five years ago, and we need to talk about that."

Four or five years ago? When he was the buddy while she pined after Eric? He did not want to be back there. He did not want to talk about being back there. And he could tell how uncomfortable she was bringing it up. He wasn't going to make her let him down gently. "All right," he said. "I get it." He picked up the press. "Your hands are clean now. Why don't you write down some questions for Friday while I finish these? Then we'll be done faster."

15

Ella's voice came through the phone hesitantly. Ruth had called her as soon as she got home from Gabriel's, and Ella wasn't sure yet if the agitation was good or bad. "What's up, Ruth?"

"Ella!" she said again.

"I asked what's going on."

"I know," Ruth said. "Do you have a minute to talk? I don't know what's going on."

"Oh, dear. Let me take my phone into my room. You can start explaining while I walk."

Ruth pulled the laces on her shoes and pushed them off as she sat on the end of her bed. "You know how I've been looking for a good time to bring up the past with Gabriel?"

Ella sucked in a breath of anticipation.

"I was so nervous, I tried several times before I actually said something."

"And what happened?"

"Oh." Ruth groaned and smacked her free hand against her bed. "I think I picked a bad moment."

"Oh, no. Did you guys like have a fight or something?"

"No. We didn't... we didn't even talk about it."

"But, um..." Ella's voice conveyed the confusion that must have been all over her face. "You said something and didn't talk about anything? Tell me exactly what happened."

"We were in his kitchen making cookies."

"What kind of antique gizmo do you use for cookies?"

Ruth laughed at the interruption. They did have a predictable pattern going. Or they had. "A cookie press. It's not antique. Quite. I don't remember when he said they were popular."

"I know I asked, but tell me about the cookie press later. What did you say about... you know?"

"Well, we were mostly having fun. Just chatting and stuff. Then we were talking about something more serious. Nothing really big. There was just this serious moment where I thought... it really looked like he was thinking about kissing me."

"That's good! Wait... that's good. How did things go bad from there?"

"I had to say something first."

"What did you say? Don't kiss me?"

"No," Ruth said, even though she could tell Ella was being sarcastic. "But I might as well have."

Ella said nothing. She was still there, just waiting for details.

"I thought we needed to clear the air before we... I need to apologize, not really for Eric because that was just a stupid misunderstanding. But afterwards... I walked away from years of friendship because it got hard. I need to say I won't do it again before Gabe and I can really have a new relationship." Ruth paused. "He didn't let me. I started to... My thoughts were jumbled so I don't remember the exact words, but I started to say that we had gotten to a point before where things were changing between us and neither of us wanted to be the one to say that and that this time, I was going to be the one to say it. And get an I'm sorry in there, too. But Gabe cut me off one sentence in and... he said we needed to work on the church group. He was... distant, businesslike, just like getting our questions for Friday was the only thing that mattered. I left as soon as we thought we had enough."

"You didn't stay for dinner?" Ella asked.

"No."

"I thought it was kind of early."

"I know I've been eating over there every week, but we hadn't made specific plans for today. And he didn't try to stop me when I said I should get going." Ruth rubbed her fingers against her forehead, trying to massage her thoughts into making sense. "Now I'm afraid I'm doing it again. Running away. I wanted to make him talk to me, but I was too confused. I'm still confused. There's a spark, lots of sparks if you ask me, so why can't he just let me say something and get it over with?"

Ella seemed to be taking a minute to decide what to say.

Ruth waited patiently. She felt a little better just having gotten a few things off her chest.

"Ruth, can I ask you something?"

"Yeah."

"Why is it so important that... I mean, why do you need to talk *first*?"

Why didn't she let him kiss her first? That was difficult to put into words. She felt it would mean more if they defined or stabilized the relationship before anything distracting happened. Because a kiss would be very distracting. She'd been sorely tempted to put off the talking at the prospect.

"Do you think maybe you feel like you need to tell him you're sorry because you want him to say it, too?" Ella asked gently.

"You mean am I holding a grudge?"

"Not a grudge really." Ella's breath buzzed against the phone as she sighed. "But you say you want him to know you won't give up so easily this time and... Well, he didn't call you either. Are you looking for assurance that he's going to stick around?"

"I don't know," Ruth said. Was she scared? Yes. But was she just plain old new relationship scared or was there something to Ella's question?

"Would you believe him?"

"Would I believe what?"

"If Gabriel said he's willing to put in the effort," Ella said, "would you believe him? Because I think if the trust isn't there, the words... And if it is, you don't need him to say it."

"Wow." Ruth was digesting the insight. "You are really smart."

"Oh, it's easy to say these things when it's someone else's relationship," Ella said dismissively. "Sometime when you're not having a crisis, we can talk about how smart I was with Adam."

"Adam who?"

"I think you can guess."

"Are you telling me you dated my brother?" Ruth was shocked that hadn't come up before. "How do I not know that?"

"We never dated." Ella's tone shifted from laughing at herself to very serious. "Do not tell him I said anything. And you and I can talk about it some other time."

"I think we're gonna have to."

"What are you going to do about Gabriel though?"

"Good question," Ruth said. "I'm not giving up. I guess on Friday I'll make sure we're still seeing each other on Sunday. It might be hard to wait that long, but that will give me time to think about exactly... We're going to talk next Sunday no matter what. There will be communication even if it's awful."

"That's the spirit. But why would it be awful?"

"I don't know. I'm just confused enough that I don't know what to expect."

****

Friday arrived with surprising speed. Work was a good distraction. Ruth watched a movie at her parents' house Thursday evening. She'd sent Gabe a couple of texts during the week, casual but deliberate texts. Twice she'd taken the time to sit down and compose a thought on their upcoming meeting. She wanted to remind him of her presence, to keep a thread of connection that they could work with.

She picked up Ella on her way to the church. Carpooling was good even if walking would have been better, environmentally speaking. It wasn't better for comfort. There was an expectation of frost and the night breeze was sharp. This time they were the first to arrive. They stood outside stomping their feet to keep warm while Mrs. Donnelly unlocked the doors. The tables and chairs could be arranged without discussion so they went straight to work.

Isaac and Jessica came in with Gabe. He was chatting with them, but his eyes quickly found Ruth. He flashed a smile before he returned his attention to Isaac.

Something in Ruth's chest jumped at the smile. It was a strong and involuntary reaction, not to Gabe's mere presence but the fact that seeing her seemed to make him happy. Maybe he was only glad to have the help of his coleader, but she hoped it was more.

Another young man walked in behind them. Ruth felt that she knew him from somewhere but not a previous meeting. It was definitely his first time there. She moved closer as he shook hands with Isaac. He introduced himself as Luke. That name was familiar, too. How did she know him?

The man had a high but smooth forehead and a dark, impressively full beard. He reached out a hand to Ruth. Instead of his name, he said, "Standard cheeseburger to go, right?"

She smiled as recognition took hold. She'd never seen him without the green shirt and white apron that was the Burger Brothers uniform. "Otherwise known as Ruth Ziebert," she said.

"Good to know. I'm Luke Wasserman."

"Welcome. Come have a seat." Ruth waved him towards the chairs where Ella was sitting. "That's Ella," she added.

He nodded. Then he moved to take the seat next to Ella. Ruth took the one on her other side, for which Ella looked grateful. There was a bit of small talk, mostly Isaac sharing with Luke what to expect from the meeting.

At 7 o'clock, there were still only six people. There hadn't been more than seven since the week Eric came. Ruth actually preferred the more intimate size, but she worried Mrs. Donnelly would decide it wasn't worth her time to continue the ministry with so few participants.

Gabriel flipped open a notebook. All mouths closed and all eyes turned to him. He laughed. "That was a surprisingly effective attention getter."

"They know you so well," Ruth said.

"Really?" He put his hands together. "What prayer am I going to start with?"

At least three people said, "The Our Father," at the same time.

Gabriel raised his eyebrows skeptically. He began with, "Lord, guide our discussion today. Help us to grow closer to you while we treat each other with respect and kindness. For this we pray, Our Father…"

The rest joined in, all of them with big smiles or stifled giggles.

For a moment, Ruth wondered if it was wrong to laugh

during a prayer. But why couldn't there be joy in talking to God?

"Today's topic is St. Christopher, who was not actually named Christopher," Gabriel said. "He was given the name because it means Christ-bearer. And I think we had a question about names before we really talk about him." He looked expectantly at Ruth.

"Yes," she said. "We had a question that's a little vague, but… Names have meanings and they also gain various associations and we wanted to ask if any of you have any particularly positive or negative feelings about your names or maybe a nickname you've had. Like I, for example, get tired of hearing that Ruth is an old person name."

"You know what gets old?" Luke sucked in a few loud breaths. "Luke, I am your father."

Jessica seemed to laugh the hardest. "Do people say that to you all the time?"

"Not all the time," he said, shaking his head. "It's just that everyone who does expects me to laugh as though it's the first time."

There were a few sympathetic groans.

"At least that's funny, or at least not offensively funny," Isaac said. "Sometimes people take the liberty of shortening my name to Ike. And then they laugh as though that's a funny name. Why is it okay to call me something that amuses you?"

"I don't think anyone means to be insulting," Jessica said. She took his hand at the same time. "I think you just have a way of inviting people to be comfortable. Comfortable enough to give you a buddy nickname."

Isaac smiled and squeezed her hand. He looked thoroughly unconvinced but happy to have his wife believe it. "Nevertheless," he said, "Ike is not an approved nickname."

Ruth bit back a smile as he finished with a glare in her direction.

"That's interesting," Gabriel said. "Very few people have ever shortened my name to Gabe so now I'm wondering if that says something about me. Even my parents call me Gabriel more often than not."

It seemed no one wanted to take a guess. Ruth actually found herself wondering what it said about her that she was one of those few. "Does Gabe bother you?" she asked.

He shrugged. "It doesn't bother me when someone shortens it or that most people don't."

Ruth felt something in his response, something she couldn't explain. He didn't give her a significant look. He didn't say when *you* shorten it. Somehow, she just knew he was thinking of her and that it not only didn't bother him, he liked that she took that liberty with his name.

"Ruth?"

She realized it was not the first time her brother tried to get her attention. "Sorry. What?"

"I think we're ready for another question," Isaac said.

"Oh, right, um…" Ruth smiled at everyone to apologize for letting her mind wander, though she couldn't actually regret the side trip. "Actually, I think Gabriel was going to tell us more about St. Christopher first."

Gabriel copied her apologetic smile. Then he mumbled, "We're really professional today, aren't we?" before he addressed the group. "The man who is now known as St. Christopher lived in what is now known as Turkey. He joined a religious order and was a large man. Apparently, he was unusually tall and strong. He was given the task of helping people cross a nearby river by carrying them on his shoulders."

"Why wasn't he given the task of building a bridge?" Luke asked.

"I don't know," Gabe said.

Ruth said, "We asked the same question."

Gabriel used the interruption to scan his notes. "So anyway, there's a legend associated with this job that one day Christopher carried a boy across who seemed to get heavier and heavier until he could barely carry him. When they made it across, the child revealed himself to be Jesus and gave him the name Christopher. Even if this is a false legend, I think we can see the obvious metaphor of seeing Christ in all the people he did carry." He turned to Ruth to take over.

"This might be a hard question," Ruth said. "But we wanted to turn this upside down. Usually, when we think of 'whatsoever you do,' we're thinking about giving food to the hungry or something else helpful. But the opposite is also true. When we do wrong to each other, we do that to Christ. Is there an area of your life where it would help to remember this? Or a specific time you wish you had remembered it?"

There were a few raised eyebrows in the room. It was a difficult, and personal, question. "Maybe we don't have to answer this one out loud," Ruth said. "Just give it a little thought."

"I can say something," Jessica said. "This question makes me think of... well, the way I let my guard down with the people closest to me. At school all day I'm working hard to treat all my kids and my coworkers with respect and kindness no matter what. Then I sometimes come home and let out all my frustration on Isaac just because I know he'll love me anyway. That's not treating him like Christ, or the way I would want to treat Christ. Shouldn't the people who love me be getting my best and not my worst?"

"Fortunately, your worst is still pretty wonderful." Isaac gazed at her sappily.

The moment was interrupted by Sebastian's entrance. "Sorry I'm late," he said. He walked towards the empty chair between Luke and Jessica. He froze at the sight of Luke.

Luke was clearly just as tense.

Gabriel made a quick introduction, though that didn't seem to be the problem.

"Have a seat," Jessica said warmly.

Sebastian thanked her and did as she asked.

Isaac looked at Ruth. "Maybe you could repeat the question to catch Sebastian up?"

Ruth nodded, but that seemed like a terrible idea. Kayla and her friends had responded to Sebastian's presence like juicy gossip. Luke was looking at him as though the man did not deserve to be alive. Restating a question that involved showing love to everyone was going to make all of them really, really uncomfortable. More so than they already were.

"Actually, I think we covered it," she said. "We're talking about St. Christopher today, Sebastian, who is sometimes invoked for safe travels because of stories about him carrying people across a river. Our next question has to do with... I might be wrong, but I think St. Christopher medals are some of the most popular religious items. How is wearing one of these different than carrying a rabbit's foot? Because I know there are people who would say it's not different."

"I like that question," Isaac said, and maybe not only because he approved of her moving on. "I think some people are guilty of using devotions as superstitions, though not always intentionally. How do we avoid falling into that trap?"

Sebastian inhaled slowly, pulling attention towards him. He

seemed to be assembling a thought to contribute. "I think one thing to keep in mind is to make sure you're not attributing any power to the item itself. If you pack a St. Christopher medal on a trip because it will remind you to lean on God if any difficulties arise, that's one thing. If you feel that you're somehow safer with the medal than without, that's... something else."

"Right." Isaac nodded. "It's about remembering who has the ultimate power. Superstitions have a way of transferring power from God. Like sometimes you'll see a baseball player making a Sign of the Cross before he steps up to the plate." He paused and held his hands up defensively. "And I'm not talking about any particular player here. I'm just saying that there's a difference between saying a quick prayer that God helps you do your best and believing that remembering to make the gesture will help you. That's giving yourself power that only God has."

Ruth found it more difficult than usual to appreciate her brother's brilliance. She was sure she wasn't the only one distracted by Luke's continued hostility.

He hadn't uncrossed his arms since Sebastian sat down. His jaw was set so tightly they could almost hear it clenching. Finally, he said, "I can't sit here." He stood and walked out, leaving a frighteningly awkward silence in his wake.

It stretched on as Ruth stared at the floor in front of her. She was just trying not to hold her breath. Then she felt Gabe lean over her shoulder. He offered a reassuring smile as he pointed to the next question.

The conversation was slow to restart, but it did. They mostly had a good discussion. During the rest of the meeting, however, Ruth sensed occasional glances both at the empty chair and the man next to it. No one completely relaxed.

They were cleaning up and Ruth was pushing a chair back to

its table when Sebastian addressed the elephant in the room. Isaac was on his other side, and he looked between her and her brother as he said, "If he comes back next week, I won't stay."

"Sebastian, you don't have to do that," Isaac said.

"Why? Because I was here first?" He gave only half a smile with his sarcasm.

Ruth had actually been thinking along those lines, as childish as it was. "You shouldn't leave," she said simply.

"Thank you for including me. I will keep coming as long as it doesn't cause trouble. I just want you to know I'll spare you from having to ask me to leave the group."

"I wouldn't do that."

"I know," he said. "That's why I'll bow out."

Ruth didn't know how to reply to that. Luckily, Sebastian didn't expect one. He simply said goodbye, including Ella with his eyes, and left with Isaac and Jessica.

"That was... strange?" Ella said. "Or maybe it was strange that it wasn't strange?" She looked as though she knew she wasn't making any sense.

Perhaps the strangest thing was that Ruth still understood her. Week after week, Sebastian acted like a nice guy, not someone who started bar fights. Nothing they knew about him was lining up with what they knew about him. Thoughts of Sebastian disappeared as Ruth noticed another nice guy was no longer in the room. "Where's Gabe?" she asked.

"He left as soon as the tables were unfolded." Ella glanced out the door. "He didn't say anything to you?"

"No. I wanted to confirm that we're still planning on Sunday."

"Well, you have to plan sometime," Ella said.

"I guess." Ruth closed the door behind her as they met Mrs.

Donnelly in the hall. They did need to plan sometime, but it unsettled Ruth to not know when.

16

Ruth tried not to think that Gabriel had left the Friday meeting in a hurry to avoid her. The thought kept trying to invade her head anyway. It didn't help that she hadn't gotten a coherent reply. She'd texted him when she got home to ask about Sunday. The response she got Saturday morning said, "I need to check something first."

She stared at it for a full minute, trying to figure out if a typo could have made it more annoying than he intended. She couldn't spot one. The unsettled feeling was pushed to the back of her mind by irritation. He could check whatever he needed to check, and maybe start making sense while he was at it, and she'd catch him after church Sunday morning to cement their usual afternoon appointment.

When Ruth didn't see Gabe at church, she wondered if he went to a different Mass. That thought she didn't want to think was back. Why would he avoid his regular Mass time other than to avoid someone who would also be there?

Maybe he was sick. A fever would let him off the hook for almost everything. The delay in fixing plans, the vague text, missing church, even rushing out on Friday might have been because he was coming down with a nasty bug. Ruth didn't want to wish him sick though. And it wouldn't explain the way he shut her out the previous weekend.

Ruth changed into nice, comfy yoga pants and an old high school sweatshirt. It hadn't left her closet in years, but she felt like remembering. She felt like reminding Gabe of good times, if she saw him. Her phone was still silent on the subject. As she held it, she felt a strong temptation to send several snide messages about whether or not he'd checked something yet. She brushed the impulse aside and simply sent a text that said, "Let me know if I should be there at three."

Then she set the phone on her dresser. If she took it to her parents' house, she'd be looking at it constantly. If she left it here, she'd return to a message that told her to come on over. No worries or fuss in the meantime. She almost believed that.

It turned out that Joseph was sick. That's what he'd told their mom, and no one had any reason to suspect *he* was avoiding anyone. Only Isaac and Jessica were there for lunch. The meal was still good and the conversation filling. Isaac asked Ruth if she wanted to shoot some hoops after.

A familiar scent wafted through the crisp fall air. "Someone's burning leaves," she said.

Isaac nodded. He stood under the hoop tossing the ball between his hands. He seemed to be waiting for something.

Ruth made a show of looking for other players. There was no one around. "Are you ready?" she asked.

"Uh..." He dribbled a few times. "Yeah, okay. Let's play."

There was something weird about his hesitation, but Ruth put it out of mind as she caught the ball. Along with a few other things she was trying not to dwell on. The physical activity helped. Ruth felt more relaxed than she had in several days and began to enjoy herself.

She was laughing over a particularly wayward shot when Jessica came out to collect her husband. "Are you ready, Isaac?"

"No," he said, and looked suddenly guilty. "We're not... finished."

"Oh. I'll wait in the car." She waved at Ruth with an unusual amount of sympathy.

Unusual because Ruth didn't know anything was wrong. She and Isaac were not keeping score so there was nothing to finish either. She would have guessed something was up even without the knowing looks that passed between her brother and sister-in-law.

Isaac tucked the ball under his arm and stepped closer to Ruth.

"Why aren't we finished?" she asked.

He put the ball back in front of himself and spun it between his hands.

Ruth took the ball away to stop his fidgeting. "Why aren't we finished?" she asked again.

Isaac closed his eyes and said, "Are you and Gabriel having some sort of problem?"

Whatever Ruth had been expecting, that wasn't it. The only problem she had with Gabriel was that she didn't know if there was a problem. She did not want to discuss that with her brother. Everything about his manner said Isaac didn't want to discuss it either. It was disconcerting that he would bring up something that he so clearly didn't want to talk about. "Why do you ask?" Ruth said.

"He, uh, he called me yesterday," Isaac said.

"And told you what?"

"Nothing," he said quickly. "Nothing about you or..." He looked at the basketball like he wanted to squeeze it while he talked. "He asked me if I would take over leading the young adult group with you."

Gabe wanted out? He wanted to stop spending his Sunday

afternoons with her? Ruth fought the swell of emotions to keep a neutral expression in front of her brother. "What did you say?"

"Well, I told him I'd have to talk to you first, that I'd work with you if that's what you want." He paused to imply the question he didn't put into words.

Ruth didn't know how to answer. It wasn't what she wanted. Not at all. But if Gabe didn't want to work with her...

"You can think about it," Isaac said. He was already turning away from her and the awkward silence she was creating. "Just let me know by Friday if you want my help. I can stop by a little before the meeting to throw something together." He got out of there so fast he probably didn't even notice that she didn't say goodbye.

Ruth didn't notice until after he left. She just stood there watching him get into his car and drive away. She forgot she was holding a basketball until she got into her tiny house and realized she had nowhere to put it. She dropped it into a corner to deal with later. That was exactly what she felt like doing. She wanted to curl into a ball in a corner somewhere and just be for a while, not thinking about anything.

She picked up her phone. A mindless game seemed like a perfect distraction. But there was a message from Gabe. He'd sent her a text that said, "I'll still be there on Friday."

He was still going to be part of the group. He wanted to stay in the group as long as he didn't have to work with Ruth to do it. And he didn't have the guts to tell her that directly. Ruth went from sad to mad faster than anyone could come up with that rhyme.

She had half a mind to march over to his place and hash out a few things. It was pretty easy to convince herself which half of her mind was the rational one. She stuffed her phone in her pocket and grabbed her car keys.

Gabriel's car was parked on the street in front of his apartment. Ruth drove past it once before she circled back and parked behind it. There would be no chickening out. She was holding on to enough anger to fuel her walk up to his front door.

Three quick pounds with the side of her fist and one deep breath later, she felt much calmer. They were going to talk. She may not enjoy the conversation, but whatever Gabe said had to be better than guessing what the heck he was thinking. The only explanation that made sense to Ruth was that all the sparks and tender moments of the last two months had been thoroughly one-sided.

And that didn't make sense because she just didn't believe it. Even if it was true, if Gabe could only offer her friendship, then it was up to her to decide if she could live with that. He didn't get to take that decision away. He was going to admit to her face how he felt about her. If he ever answered the door.

"Gabriel?" she called. She knocked again, no pounding just a regular knock.

Still the door remained closed. She didn't hear any movement behind it.

Ruth looked up and down the street and saw no one. She sighed and rested her forehead against the doorframe with her mouth aimed at the crack. "I'm going to say what I came to say even if I have to do it through the door," she said. But what exactly did she want to say? She'd showed up determined to make him talk.

"Gabe, I... I don't want to do this group thing with Isaac. Not because I... Well, I'd just rather do it with you. We've had so much fun, haven't we? Why are you trying to quit on me? Is it...

Can you tell how I feel about you? Is it obvious that even after all the years we were apart, I still love you as much as I ever did? If you only want to be friends, I can try. I don't know if I can because right now I'm still hoping for more. You have to tell me there's no hope before I can know if I can... What do you want from me, Gabe? I regret so much that I gave up so easily last time. I will at least try, I will work to make this relationship what you want if you'll only tell me what you want." Ruth wiped a tear that frustration had pushed out. She felt as though she could use a hug even more than words. "Please open the door."

More silence greeted her request. He must not be home. Ruth had assumed that all along. She wasn't sure she'd have had the courage to pour her heart out to the crack in the door if she thought anyone was on the other side.

She jumped backwards as a door creaked open. It wasn't Gabriel's but the one on the other side of the building. Jojo exited. He appeared to be wearing the same layers as the last time Ruth saw him. He pulled a key out of his sleeve, one of his sleeves, to lock the door behind him. It was attached by a piece of yarn to the sleeve or something inside it. He was pushing it back in place when he noticed Ruth. He froze for a second and then continued to where the two sidewalks met.

Ruth offered a greeting by way of a smile and nod. She was a little talked out.

Jojo pointed between her and Gabriel's front door with his eyebrows raised in question.

"Yeah, I came to... visit Gabriel," she said. "I don't think he's home though."

He pumped his arms like he was running.

"Oh, I bet that's where he is." She glanced at the car. It made sense that Gabriel could be out jogging.

Jojo nodded briefly. He looked at his own door as though deciding if he might be forgetting something. Then he turned and walked away.

There was one stone step in front of Gabriel's front door. Ruth sat on it to wait for him. The cold seeped through her pants and made her shiver. She took out her phone and considered texting him that she was at his place. If he was jogging though, he wouldn't have his phone with him. And knowing she was waiting might not make him hurry back. There was an annoying thought.

Ruth put her head down and looked at the sidewalk. There was a crack where it'd been pushed up by a tree root. A dry leaf was flapping, snagged on a corner by that crack. She watched it moving in the breeze, then let her eyes travel back and forth across the root sticking out of the ground nearby. After nearly an hour, Ruth could no longer pretend that the leaf, the sidewalk, the tree root, the breeze or anything else was keeping her from being bored beyond reason. Not to mention freezing.

She stood up and hugged herself. Gabriel could have jogged to his parents' house or a friend's house or the library or... there were a lot of places a person could reach on foot in a small town. It was possible he might be gone another hour or even two. Ruth was not giving up. Getting in her car to go back home did not mean she was giving up. She and Gabe were going to have a serious conversation. It just wasn't going to happen that afternoon.

17

Gabriel was at his parents' house. He'd been out jogging and ended up there on what he knew would prove to be a regrettable whim. There were a lot of reasons he suspected regret. His mom had stopped herself from asking him a question about ten times since he'd arrived, and he knew they were all about Ruth.

"Why aren't you with Ruth right now?"

"Shouldn't you be planning questions with Ruth?"

"Why didn't you bring Ruth with you?"

"How long before you and Ruth are engaged anyway?"

He knew all the questions on her mind. He did not know how to answer any of them. It was therefore best that she was keeping them to herself. So far.

Unfortunately, she was asking questions even when she wasn't asking questions. She'd talked about a recent visit with Ruth's parents, leaving not-so-subtle pauses here and there for him to insert anything he might want to add about that family. Now she was going on and on about her bible study and the cookies he had made for it.

"I got several compliments on those cookies," she said. "And each time I was able to say that it was actually my son who made them." There was a tiny break after the word son where she had clearly thought about adding "and Ruth" but didn't.

Gabriel did not fill in the gap for her.

"I told them how I didn't even have to ask, how my adult son simply volunteered to do something nice for his mother."

Because he knew Ruth would enjoy helping him, which he also did not say out loud.

"Of course, they all thought it was so sweet of you. It wasn't too much trouble, was it?" His mom smiled innocently while she was practically begging him to admit he volunteered the time to spend it with Ruth.

"You're welcome, Mom," he said.

She frowned at the tone that he knew implied she was mostly welcome to stop talking about it.

He might have tried to appease her with a more sincere comment but was interrupted by the sound of the back door opening. Another reason that coming over had been a mistake. When Gabriel agreed to stay for dinner, his mom immediately called his brother and insisted the whole family should eat together.

Their dad looked up from the book he was reading as Eric entered the room. There was a bit of silent nodding to acknowledge each other as he sat down. Gabriel prepared himself to appear unaffected by any news Eric might have.

"So what have you been up to, Eric?" His mom beamed at each of the three men, one of whom had gone back to his book.

"Same old, same old," Eric said with a shrug. "Work, sleep, work, sleep."

"That's not all you do," his mom insisted. "Haven't you been enjoying the new young adult group at St. Jude's?" She glanced at Gabriel with a plea for confirmation.

Gabriel kept his mouth shut. Eric was on his own.

"I, uh… haven't really been going much," Eric said.

"Why not?" She sounded concerned. "After all the work your brother has been putting in?"

With Ruth. His mom didn't add those words, but Gabriel could feel her thinking that he'd been putting in the work with Ruth. That's why it hadn't felt like work and likely why her question to Eric carried only a wet-noodle admonishment.

Eric didn't say much to defend himself. He only said, "I don't know."

"That's not a reason." Their mom let out a disgusted snort before she turned her attention to her younger son. "Gabriel, are there any young women coming on Fridays?"

He nodded because they all knew Ruth was there. She was a woman.

That motherly gaze kept boring into him for more information. After a minute of silence, she said, "What about Ruth's friend, Ella?"

"She's there," Gabriel confirmed.

It was enough to get her to turn back to Eric. "Didn't Ella Sweet go to school with you? She was in your class, right?"

"Yeah," Eric said.

Again she waited for more information that wasn't forthcoming. "And?" she prompted.

Eric just shrugged at her.

"Tell me who all was there this last Friday." She was looking at Gabriel again.

He sighed and prepared to list off the names.

"Mom," Eric said, "I don't think the point of a church group is to pick up a woman."

"Of course it's not the point," she said. "But that doesn't mean it can't be a nice side effect. Or an incentive to get you there."

Eric sent an annoyed look at Gabriel. It seemed to be a request for help in redirecting the conversation. Gabriel simply reflected the annoyance. He knew it wasn't Eric's fault that Ruth preferred him. The usual eye banter they shared over their mother's nagging was still beyond him at the moment.

"Well, what have you been talking about in the group anyway?" She began to move on without nudging.

"Saints," Gabriel said.

She closed her eyes. "I know that. Which saints?"

Now Gabriel had a shrug for her.

She stared at him impatiently. Her eyes flickered to her husband, then Eric, then back. They probably stayed on Gabriel most because Eric was always the quiet one. She expected more conversation from Gabriel. He started to feel guilty about his belligerent silence, but he just did not feel like talking.

"Have there been any…" Her voice trailed off as she shook her head in frustration. "I guess I'll go start on dinner." She left the room muttering something about pulling teeth.

There were some magazines in a rack at the end of the couch. Gabriel reached over and pulled one out at random. He flipped through a few pages without looking at them. The crinkle of each turn was the only sound in the room.

Until Eric said, "What's up with you today?"

"Nothing." Gabriel looked up for a second, then back at the magazine he wasn't reading.

Eric gave up. He tipped his head against the back of the armchair and closed his eyes.

"Hey, I'm making chicken parmigiana, and I just realized I'm out of pasta to go with it." Their mom's voice came into the room ahead of her. As she appeared in the doorway, she added, "Can one of you run to Seymour's and get me a box of spaghetti noodles?"

Gabriel was on his feet before she finished talking. He really needed to get out of that house, if only for a few minutes. He borrowed his mom's car to run the errand faster.

Seymour's was always very bright. That was what Gabriel noticed as he entered. The lights seemed to be cranked up to an unnecessary wattage while signs everywhere said things in bold colors. He blinked against the sensory assault and made his way to the pasta aisle.

What kind of noodles did his mom usually buy? He scanned the brands and picked up the one with the most familiar packaging. Walking out of the aisle, he bumped into – not quite literally – two women he recognized.

They stopped as they also recognized him. Sort of. "St. Jude's, right?" one of them said.

He nodded. He knew the other one was Kayla and that her friend had been to the one meeting with her. But he couldn't remember her name. "Gabriel Chadwick," he said, hoping a name would be supplied.

"That's right," Kayla said. "You're the guy who's dating Adam's sister."

"No," he said.

The two of them exchanged a knowing look. He didn't care to know what they thought they knew. He was about to step away with a generic pleasantry when Kayla opened her mouth to say something to him.

"Did your group fall apart without us?" She smiled, but there was something in the question that sounded almost rhetorical.

"We're still meeting every Friday," he said. "Both of you would be welcome to join us."

They looked at each other again. "Adam actually thought he might want to go back, but obviously." Kayla finished the sentence as though she had finished the sentence.

Her friend nodded in agreement.

"Have a nice day," Gabriel said, moving towards the checkout line.

Seymour's was popular that Sunday. It was popular with customers anyway, not so much with employees. Maria Daniels was the only person behind a register, and she already had four or five people waiting when Gabriel got in line. He checked his watch and hoped his mom didn't already have water boiling.

"Oh, I love these," he heard Mrs. Daniels say. She had one of those voices that couldn't be kept down. Not that she tried. She was holding a bag of pita chips that she'd just scanned. "These are so good with a tuna dip."

The customer replied in a softer voice.

"You need the right kind of mayo. I'll tell you, the store brand is actually pretty good. Then add a little vinegar and a little sugar." She picked up another item and had a suggestion for how to eat that, too.

Gabriel sensed someone stopping behind him. When he turned back to offer a commiserating smile, he saw Kayla and her friend again. They both had their phones about eight inches from their faces and were avoiding or oblivious to the attempt at eye contact. He didn't bother to feel ignored.

He let his attention drift over the items on the impulse buy rack. No. No. Nothing was triggering an impulse to buy. The 3 Musketeers did look good though. He used to love those. He remembered the last time he went trick-or-treating with Ruth. If he remembered correctly, they were in seventh grade. She'd traded him all eight of her 3 Musketeers for one of his peanut butter cups.

It wasn't the generous trade it sounded like. Ruth hated 3 Musketeers. She'd threatened to toss all of hers in the trash if he didn't give up the full-size peanut butter cup. It was funny that something that had annoyed him in the past made him smile in the present.

The line had moved so that only two people remained in front of him. Mrs. Daniels was still treating her job like a hobby, like it was everyone else's hobby, too. "Oh, I've been meaning to try this new barbeque flavor," she said. "Is it any good?"

Again the customer's response was lost to a normal speaking volume.

"You'll have to tell me next time you're in here." Mrs. Daniels smiled. "They make a whole grain version. Did you see it?"

Gabriel could probably make out what the customers were saying if he really listened. But he wasn't listening. Mrs. Daniels' voice was just too loud to tune out. Until she said, "I can send someone to pick one up for you."

Then he did try to hear the response. The current customer was Cindy, a 30ish woman with dark hair. She had three small white dogs that Gabriel sometimes saw her walking when he was out jogging. She was telling Mrs. Daniels that whatever she'd offered to get wasn't worth the trouble.

Unfortunately, the cashier was not easily dissuaded from being helpful. A groan came from the back of the line. Gabriel shifted the box to his other hand to pull his vibrating phone from his pocket. Perhaps the visit with his parents was not as spontaneous as he wanted to believe. The phone would not be in his pocket if he'd really expected to be gone no longer than a typical run. He figured the text was his mom asking if he'd gotten lost.

He was wrong. The text said, "Ruth doesn't want me to take

over. I'm not getting in the middle." Isaac was refusing to lead the group with Ruth. Gabriel was disappointed but not terribly surprised. He'd expected Isaac to say he was too busy though, not wanting to take on anything new with a baby on the way. That was a respectable excuse. His words about not getting in the middle insinuated that Gabriel and Ruth were involved in some petty spat.

There was nothing petty about wanting to avoid spending time alone with a beautiful woman who was dating someone else. Unless...

Was she dating someone else? He'd been assuming Ruth and Eric were going to start dating because she wanted to date him. But what if Eric didn't want to date her? What if he was actually skipping the Friday meetings to avoid coming between Gabriel and Ruth?

Gabriel couldn't say he was relieved at the thought. It'd be nice if he could say he was mature enough to want Ruth to be happy even if it was with someone else. But it likely had more to do with wanting to direct any anger at the situation towards Eric.

Either way, the idea of her staying single brought up an important question. Would Gabriel still have a chance? If he spent enough time with her, would she eventually settle for him? And could he live with being the second choice?

There were a lot of ifs on her side. For his part, there wasn't anything to debate. He'd jump at any chance to make the relationship closer.

"You forget the sauce?" Mrs. Daniels asked.

It was finally Gabriel's turn to pay. He smiled politely and pulled out a credit card. "I only need the noodles."

"What about meatballs?" she asked. "You can't have spaghetti without meatballs."

"My mom is cooking."

"Does she use a chunky sauce or more of a marinara?"

Gabriel had his card hovering over the reader, but she hadn't pushed the button to let it accept the card. The noodles were being held hostage by the conversation. Someone farther back in line was shifting his weight impatiently. Gabriel almost said something rude to end the conversation, but he realized that causing a scene would not be faster.

If he had to talk, it might as well be pleasant. "She still makes a smooth sauce because my brother and I used to complain about the chunks when we were kids," he said. "I think I'd like to try a heartier sauce though."

Her whole face lit up as she smiled *and* pushed the button to let him pay. "I think it's fascinating the way our taste buds change as we age."

"What do you eat that you used to refuse?"

"Oh, lima beans. I love them now." She tore off the receipt. "Do you need a bag?"

"No, thanks," he said. "Have a nice day." He smiled as he walked away and felt that he wasn't completely faking it. How had a long line improved his mood, even incrementally?

The dark cloud edged closer to Gabriel's sky as he sat at a table with his brother. Eric's presence reminded him of things he couldn't control and possibilities he didn't know if he should hope for. The uncertainty was the problem, not Eric. Uncertainty he could do something about. He could ask Eric. The wrong answer might make Eric the problem, but that was a bridge best left uncrossed for the moment.

Gabriel did his best to chat with his mom. It wasn't her fault everything she said made him think of Ruth. Once the meal was cleaned up, Eric said he was heading home.

Gabriel followed him out the door.

"Do you want a ride?" Eric asked.

"No, thanks. Are you going to start dating Ruth again?"

Eric stopped walking. He looked at Gabriel as though he didn't recognize him. "What are you talking about?"

This wasn't a discussion about anyone's feelings. It was a simple fact-finding mission. "Are you going to start dating Ruth again?" he repeated, as casually as he could manage.

"No. Couldn't do it *again* anyway. You wanna ask me any other stupid questions?"

"You forgot your pumpkins!" Their mom was struggling to get out the back door with a large gourd under each arm. Both guys rushed to help her and to get away from any other stupid questions.

Gabriel said, "I guess I might take you up on the ride now." Running home in the cold would have been fine. Running home with a pumpkin seemed like a bad idea. They didn't talk in the car. Gabriel was hoping Eric had already forgotten what he'd asked. Eric might actually forget, or at least assume it was an impulsive joke.

It would be more difficult to drive from Gabriel's mind, particularly that part about again. Was it possible that it was someone else who came between them years ago? And was that person more completely out of the picture? Had his jealous mind overestimated the number of times Ruth had mentioned his brother recently?

He and Eric managed a silent nodding farewell as he got out with the pumpkin. There was a new text as he emptied his pockets on his counter. Ruth didn't want to wait until Friday to plan. She wanted to know if she could come over after work on Monday.

No matter what had happened in the past, no matter how low the chances of anything good in the future, Gabriel couldn't deny

that he wanted to see her. He wanted to see Ruth. He sat down
with the phone to make that happen.

18

"What did Isaac say?" Ella whispered back.

"He, um..." Ruth glanced up as Mr. Sweet appeared in the doorway.

He leaned against the frame and smoothed out his tie as he crossed his ankles. "Sorry to interrupt," he said. He was smiling and didn't look the least bit sorry. It wasn't the first time that Monday he'd interrupted a hushed conversation. He confirmed that Ella and Ruth had completed a few tasks, then he reminded them he was about to leave the office for an appointment. "Plenty of time for whispering while I'm gone." He kept smiling as he returned to his office.

Ella raised her eyebrows to repeat the question still in the air.

"Isaac said he was glad I was going to keep trying to lead the class, but he had this smug tone that suggested he was talking about something between me and Gabriel. I mean, I'm not even the one who wanted to back out of leading."

"What did he say to Gabriel?"

"I don't know," Ruth said, still whispering. "But I hope he kept his insinuations out of it."

Ella smiled, then rolled her eyes as she answered the phone that interrupted.

Ruth half typed up an email and half listened as Ella spoke to a customer who insisted he'd paid a bill he hadn't paid. The man had unbelievable luck with the post office losing his checks. As shy as Ella could be in person, she didn't seem to have any trouble telling the man on the phone exactly what needed to happen for his policy to be renewed.

Mr. Sweet left the office as she finished the call. Ella jotted a note on the corresponding file before she turned back to Ruth. "Now we can really talk," she said. "What time is Gabriel expecting you tonight?"

"Seven."

"Hmm." She tipped her head. "Do you think you can have everything settled by 7:05?"

"I doubt it." Ruth refused to laugh at the optimism. "I can't even decide what order we need to discuss all the things we need to discuss."

Ella winced.

"What?"

"Are you sure you need to discuss everything?" She flagged the word discuss with annoying finger quotes. "Your *we need to talk* attitude might be what's scaring him away."

"We do need to talk," Ruth said. "You make it sound like I'm threatening to communicate with him. And I have never used that foreboding tone."

"I know." Ella flashed a smile as a meager bit of contrition for the teasing. "What were you saying about having to talk about things in a certain order?"

Ruth shook her head to rattle some thoughts around. "Well," she said, "we have to come up with questions for Friday. That's why we're getting together so I wonder if we should get that out of the way first, but I doubt I'll be able to concentrate with other stuff hanging over us. I sort of want to start by talking through how everything fell apart before since that's been, you know, festering the longest. But I'm dying to give him a piece of my mind about the way he tried to get Isaac to take over without even telling me. That's almost certainly going to be the first thing out of my mouth. And what if I start with that and things go badly? If I yell at him for backing out and then find out he only wants to be friends… then I might want to back out. Is it better to make that hard for me to do or… Things could go really badly."

Ella smiled sympathetically. "All right. It might take until 7:10 to settle everything."

Ruth laughed and relaxed somewhat. "Am I making it too complicated?"

"Hard not to when your emotions get all tied in knots but…" Ella leaned forward as though she was about to share a secret. "Didn't you say he almost kissed you?"

A smile jumped to Ruth's face with some color at the memory. She gave a quick nod.

"Then I don't think you have anything to worry about," Ella said.

"I would have agreed with you before he tried to dump me on Isaac. Why would someone who likes me want to avoid me though?"

Ella sat back in her chair, apparently pushed there by a bit of confusion. "Time alone would give him a better chance to try again."

"That's my point," Ruth said, though she felt no satisfaction at convincing Ella of it.

Ella looked thoughtful for a moment before a conciliatory smile bloomed. "I guess that means you need to talk to him to find out."

"I know." Ruth kind of wished she had a pillow to throw at Ella for agreeing with her. Mostly, she was frustrated that she was no longer frustrated. It was an odd feeling, to find calm annoying. But after a good night's sleep and talking to Ella about the situation, Ruth couldn't get herself worked up the way she'd been on Sunday. She worried that if she went over to Gabriel's feeling peaceful, she'd be tempted not to rock the boat, tempted to leave unsaid things that should be said.

By 6:30, Ruth had already eaten dinner and brushed her teeth – because if things went well, she'd want her breath fresh – and was pacing her kitchen. It was exactly three steps across. Three small steps. Any time her stride lengthened, she walked into the sink and straightened the neatly folded towel. The nervous excitement that was building was worse than the calm. She wanted to see Gabe. And she wanted to pretend everything was fine so she could simply enjoy his company.

The feeling reminded her of all the times in high school when she thought she'd eventually marry Gabriel without ever having to admit she wanted to. It would somehow just happen. As foolish as the idea was, she wanted to grab it again and hang on.

Ruth wadded up the towel her fingers were unconsciously smoothing. What she really wanted was to stop waiting around as though Gabe would be with other patients if she arrived early. She tossed the towel into a corner and put on her shoes and jacket.

A car she didn't recognize was parked behind Gabriel's. Ruth felt a flash of worry that someone else was already enjoying his company. She shrugged it off and parked behind the red car, careful to leave plenty of room for the intruder – if it was an intruder – to get out. The idea might not have been entirely shrugged off.

There was a pumpkin on the step at Gabe's front door. It wasn't carved. A classic face with triangle eyes and zigzag mouth was drawn in black marker. And it was wearing a lime green wig cut like a frizzy mullet. Ruth was still staring at it as she knocked.

"Nice pumpkin," she said as the door opened.

Gabe sighed a bit dramatically. "My mom said I had to decorate my place and gave me that. She'd already made it."

"You don't like it?"

He shrugged. "Eric got one with a scowl and devil horns and I got green hair. I just..." The words failed him, but Ruth could read his expression. He slightly preferred the one his brother got and was embarrassed that he cared even slightly.

"You're jealous of your brother's pumpkin?" she teased.

He rolled his eyes as he stepped back to let her inside. His tie was already loose, and he undid the knot completely and tossed the tie onto the sofa while Ruth set down her bag and took off her jacket.

There were books on the table as always. Ruth stepped closer and gestured to them. "I guess we should get started." She hoped that if she ignored the thousand kilowatts of awkwardness in the room it would go away. It felt like the first day she came over. Again. How had the relationship gone so far backwards? Again.

Gabriel didn't help matters. He came to the table but didn't sit down with her. He stood over her and said, "Sorry about yesterday. Making you wait."

She'd texted Gabe to arrange this Monday meeting. In one of them, Ruth mentioned how she'd sat on his porch for an hour. He'd apologized and explained how he'd ended up at his parents' house for dinner when he thought Isaac was taking over. It all seemed inconsequential at the time. Now she was suddenly embarrassed to have told him. She tried to wave away the extra apology.

He still looked guilty, but maybe he was simply uncomfortable.

Ruth was sure she was more uncomfortable with him making her look up and feel stupid about waiting around after he'd canceled their appointment. Just as suddenly as the embarrassment took hold, Ruth was able to channel some anger through it. Thankfully, it was the productive kind of anger, the kind that prodded her to get to the bottom of things. Because she realized that Gabriel seemed to be apologizing for one thing when she was upset about something else.

"What exactly are you sorry about?" she asked.

His hand froze on the back of the chair he was pulling out. "Yesterday?"

"Are you sorry that I was waiting for you? Or that you tried to quit all this on me?" She shoved one of the books off its stack. "Or that you didn't actually try to quit? You tried to get my brother to quit for you."

Gabriel's mouth twitched with a nervous smile, which he immediately squelched. "What do you want me to be sorry for?"

"Nothing."

"Nothing?" His voice and expression shared the same skepticism.

Ruth held her tongue as he slowly lowered himself into the chair. She knew her tone was accusing him of a lot more than nothing. His eyes had trepidation and sadness, but also resignation. He appeared ready to have a potentially awful conversation, and that was what she wanted. Not an awful conversation but the willingness.

"Nothing," Ruth repeated. "I don't want you to apologize for anything. I just want you to explain to me why… I mean, if you're still coming to the group, why can't you help me lead it? And if you don't want to, why did you agree in the first place?"

His quick laugh was more like a snort. "No one says no to Mrs. Donnelly."

So that was it. He never wanted to work with Ruth in the first place. He'd only been biding his time until he could back out without talking to Mrs. Donnelly, who met excuses like a wrecking ball. And Ruth had made it just as difficult for him. "Oh. I guess if... I don't want to make you do something you don't want to do. But I thought you were at least kind of enjoying..."

"It's been great."

He said great like a reflex, like he just agreed to something without listening to what it was.

"Great?" Ruth reached across the table and poked his arm. "Come on. The crazy saint stories. The food we made together. That time you caught the bread dough I kneaded right off the counter? Hasn't that been more than great?"

Gabe only nodded, but she could tell he was paying attention now. And she could tell that the sparks were not her imagination. That almost kiss had not been her imagination. There was something strong between them. And maybe that was the reason Gabe tried to quit. He was attracted to her but didn't want a relationship. That was the only thing that made sense.

Except that it didn't make sense because why not!? They had a long history of friendship. They still had similar goals for the future. Their families were pretty much counting on them getting together so there would be no objections. Unless Gabe had an objection, a grudge?

This was Ruth's opportunity to bring up that other part of their history that they'd been dodging. She was ready to say something but mentally stumbled over the right words. Should she start with an apology? An explanation? An assurance that she'd matured over the last few years? A promise that she wouldn't walk away easily?

"I talked to Eric yesterday," Gabriel said into the void her mental tripping left.

The simple statement oozed significance. He was thinking about the past, too. Ruth waited for him to say more. It might give her a clue about what he needed to hear from her.

"Just for a minute," he said, "as we were leaving Mom and Dad's."

He'd talked to Eric for a minute? Sherlock Holmes couldn't find a clue in that.

"He said, uh…" Gabe dropped his eyes to the table between them. "He said he never went out with you."

"Good." Ruth sighed with relief. When she noticed the way it made him glance back up, she added, "I mean, I'm glad he didn't think it was a date either."

"You guys were making out and neither of you wants to call it a date?"

Ruth felt herself physically pull back at this surprising accusation. "I have never… ever… *made out* with Eric."

"Then who was it?"

"Who was what?"

"The guy you were with in college."

Ruth was momentarily dumbfounded. All this time she thought they just needed to admit how stupid they were for not clearing up a simple misunderstanding. Now she didn't even know what needed to be cleared up. "First you need to tell me what you mean by 'the guy I was with' because I don't know what you're talking about."

"What do you mean by 'it wasn't a date?'"

"I had lunch with Eric," Ruth said. "A very innocent,

friendly lunch that you got mad at me about."

Gabriel shook his head at her version of events. "My roommate told me that he saw you kissing Eric outside our building."

"Your roommate was a jerk! Why would you believe anything he said?"

"Because I'd just given Eric your phone number, which you seemed pretty happy about, and then you started ignoring me. I figured you had to be spending your time with somebody."

"It wasn't Eric."

"Then who was it? Never mind. Don't tell me." He held his hand up defensively.

"It wasn't anyone," Ruth said. Thinking about how lonely she was when they'd lost touch was as draining as the circular conversation. "I missed you like crazy."

"Then why didn't you call me?"

"Because you didn't call me."

Gabriel rubbed his hand over his face. "I deserve that."

Ruth sat quietly for a minute, processing. She heard Gabe inhale as though he was about to say something. The breath came out with no words.

After a long pause, he said, "Uh, just to be clear…" Then he was quiet again.

Ruth looked up at him, wondering what might be clear.

By the expression on his face, nothing. His eyes were squinted and darting around behind his glasses. "So you didn't… And you don't…"

"Are you trying to ask me if I have a thing for Eric?" Ruth asked, suddenly amused by his inability to form a sentence.

"No," he said. "I am trying *not* to ask that."

"Well, for the record, I don't."

"Why do you talk about him all the time?"

"Do I?"

"Yes." This was one point on which Gabriel seemed crystal clear. "You've been asking me every week to get him to come on Fridays and asking me even more often why we're not seeing him on Fridays."

"Oh." Now that she thought about it, Ruth realized she'd been bugging him a lot about bugging Eric. It must have been really annoying. "Sorry," she said. "I'm just afraid Mrs. Donnelly will shut us down if we don't have enough participants."

"Did she say anything about needing a certain number?"

"No. But it must be a pain for her to bring the key over every week."

"You're right." Gabriel sat back in his chair. "I can't believe I didn't think about this before. She lives right down the street from the church. I'll ask if I can stop by and pick up the key on my way, then bring it back when we're done. It'd save her two trips, and we won't be stuck outside if we're early." He finished with a satisfied nod.

Ruth felt anything but satisfied. Mrs. Donnelly wasn't her biggest concern at the moment. As she went over everything she and Gabe talked about, she began to understand how much had been her fault. Her silence had let him believe she was dating someone else, had abandoned him to chase after someone better. All she'd had to do was open the line. They'd lost years because of her foolish pride. "I'm sorry," she said. She didn't wait for Gabe to respond. She was going to get this out. "I'm sorry I didn't call you back then. I'm sorry that I just gave up. I want you to know I won't do that again. Yes, it's taken me weeks to work up the courage to say it, but that doesn't make it less true."

"What will you not do again?"

"Give up easily."

"On what?" There was more hope in his question than question.

Ruth studied his face, his eyes that were no longer floating around but fixed on hers. It was one of those moments where nothing else seems real, where words add nothing. They both knew they'd found the best kind of friendship. Unnecessary or not, Ruth wanted to express it in words. She only managed one. "This," she whispered.

Gabriel put his hands on the table between them. She also reached out and laced her fingers through his. He leaned forward. Ruth did, too. They moved slowly closer. Until Ruth realized that the table was too wide. They couldn't kiss across it unless they vacated their chairs and while that could happen, it wouldn't feel natural. It would definitely interrupt the moment. She felt herself fighting a giggle.

Gabriel let go of one of her hands to pull a book in front of them. "By this you mean this group? You will drag me kicking and screaming back to lead with you no matter what?"

"That's exactly what I mean," Ruth said.

"Then I guess we better get started."

Ruth nodded, not reluctantly. Their fingers kept touching until it became awkward to turn pages one-handed. A topic jumped out at them quickly, only in part because the book had some good discussion questions. They sat at the table talking about other things for hours after their work was done. She noticed that he kept glancing down at the table as though he wished it wasn't in the way. Ruth knew she was doing the same thing. They couldn't stop thinking about what it had interrupted.

Finally, she had to admit that it was late. "I should go. I have to work tomorrow and everything."

"Will you come over for dinner after work?" Gabe asked. "I feel like inventing hamburgers again."

Ruth smiled at the invitation, how easily it was issued now that they'd put mistakes behind them. "Sure," she said. "That sounds great."

He stood to walk her to the door.

Ruth had a shocking amount of difficultly fitting her arms through the sleeves of her jacket. She didn't think her body had felt so uncoordinated since she was a toddler. It took two tries to get her bag all the way to her shoulder. Gabe was standing by the door watching and waiting.

She stopped closer to him than the door when she was ready to go. "Well, I guess this is goodbye until tomorrow."

He nodded. "Yeah." Moved a little closer.

Ruth was too focused on the way his eyes flickered to her mouth to see his hand come up until his fingers began to move along her chin. She startled, even as it sent a lot of tingles to a lot of places. Apparently, her lungs were included because the simple in and out of breathing suddenly required thought. Still Gabe did not erase that last foot of space. The tingles began to mix with impatience.

Gabriel came about an inch closer. Then he stepped back abruptly, dropping his hand to his side. "There is way too much buildup here."

It wasn't funny, but Ruth laughed anyway. Just enough to relieve some of the tension.

Gabe smiled, too. Then he sobered up, gave a committed nod, and kissed her. The contact was over in a few seconds. That was all it took to swell her chest with emotion. She floated out the door and all the way home.

19

Ruth was still on a new relationship high on Friday. Even though it wasn't a new relationship. Besides her family, she'd known Gabe longer than anyone. The relationship had definitely taken a new direction though. They'd spent over an hour on the phone the previous night, and it'd been difficult to hang up.

Ruth had vowed not to be too gushy around Ella. Ella was happy for her, and she wanted to keep it that way. Besides, there was something else she wanted to talk about when Ella got in her car for a ride to the church. "We're alone now," she said.

"Let me at least buckle my seat belt first."

"You just proved you can talk and buckle at the same time," Ruth protested.

Ella looked away to focus on the seat belt and failed to cover the fact that she was turning red. "You're so impatient." Her attempt to stall couldn't be more obvious.

"It's a short drive to the church." Ruth put the car in gear to begin that drive. She'd remembered while they were at work that Ella had let something slip about Adam. Ella said she'd hoped Ruth had forgotten for good, but she promised to tell her when they were very alone.

"All right," Ella said. "First you have to promise that you will never tell anyone in your family, but especially not Adam."

"You know I won't tell anyone anything that would embarrass you."

"I do. I'm stalling."

Ruth smiled. The second attempt had been less obvious than the first. "Come on, let's hear it."

"Do you remember the, um, the secret admirer notes?" Ella's voice got quieter and ended at barely a whisper.

"Oh! My! Goodness! That was you?" Adam had gotten a series of notes from a secret admirer in 11th grade. Each message had been spelled out with words cut from magazines like a ransom note. He'd never let Ruth read any of them, and she only knew they existed because people at school had been gossiping and speculating about them.

Ella had her hands covering her face, but Ruth got a glimpse of how red she was. "It's probably the stupidest thing I've ever done," she said, "and I assure you it was a short-lived crush."

"Well, I can assure you that he definitely never found out who sent them."

"Thank God for that." Ella quickly glanced up as she lowered her hands. "I actually had this fantasy at the time of how he was going to be so moved by the notes – which, by the way, were mostly quotes from poems or songs – that he'd need to find me. It sounds like something a twelve-year-old might try, and I was sixteen. Anyway, in hindsight, I'm glad the gossip got crazy. Once people were talking about the secret admirer stalker, I realized how dumb it was and stopped before I got caught."

"I have to ask," Ruth said. "How many notes did you slip into his locker because I heard everything from just once to every day for a month?"

Ella laughed. She almost looked relieved to be talking about it. "There were only three notes. I put one in every few days for...

probably a week between the first and last. People were definitely talking about it longer."

"Yeah. His friends were giving him joking notes for a while afterwards. I saw one that came in the mail that said something about 'If you want to see your heart again...' before he started ripping it up."

It was a short drive. Ruth had already pulled the car into a parking spot behind the church. She kept it running for heat and white noise to keep the conversation private. The overhead light popped on when Ella opened her door. Ruth prepared to exit as well. She noticed Joseph walking through the lot in front of them.

Ella sent her a fierce look and said, "Not a word."

There was more than one secret entrusted to Ruth.

Joseph waited for them by the door and opened it as they approached. Ella went through first with a quiet thank you. Ruth made a face at her brother as she went through. He pretended to drop the door but caught it again before it hit her.

Gabe and Isaac had already arranged the room. No one else arrived by a few minutes after seven. Ruth was grateful Mrs. Donnelly didn't see the lowest turnout yet. Mixed with more gratitude to Gabe for picking up the key – Mrs. Donnelly agreed to leave it in her mailbox from now on – was a bit of guilt. She'd been fretting about the trouble they were causing the woman for weeks, and it took someone else to point out that maybe they could do something about it.

"This is everyone?" Joseph asked.

"Jessica said she was going to come," Isaac said, "but then she fell asleep on the couch, and I didn't want to wake her."

"What about Sebastian?" Ruth asked. "Have you talked to him this week?"

"Bumped into him a few times, but we didn't talk about the

group. He said last week he would keep coming."

"I don't know." Gabriel had his notebook on his lap. He hadn't opened it yet. "I'm afraid that... unpleasantness with Luke made him decide not to come back. Maybe both of them."

There was a collective sigh as no one quite knew what to say about the... unpleasantness. After some silence, Isaac nodded to the notebook. Gabriel took the cue to start them with a prayer. Then he smiled a little self-consciously and said, "Why does the group seem so much smaller today? We've had meetings with only six or seven."

"It doesn't seem that much smaller," Ruth said.

"I kind of like the smaller... not that... I mean, this is okay." Ella looked as though she regretted speaking up.

Isaac grinned at Joseph. "I know why he thinks it's smaller."

"Me, too." The brothers shared a very smug nod. They didn't play up the twin thing often, and they still looked very little alike. But they were definitely thinking the same thought as two pairs of eyes bored into Gabriel, then flicked significantly to Ruth before going back.

Ruth was highly suspicious of whatever thought they had now that it included her. "What?" she said, with a warning they ignored.

Joseph kept smiling a disturbing smile.

Isaac said, "He knows we're watching him now."

A brief giggle came out of Ella before she squelched it.

Ruth didn't find the intimidating big brother act funny. Of course, she didn't find it intimidating either.

"We planned to talk about four saints today," Gabriel said. "The gospel writers." His eagerness to start the discussion was clearly prompted by Isaac's statement. Whether he felt threatened or simply acted threatened for the brothers' amusement, Ruth didn't know. She did know that he was looking at her to start.

"Oh, yeah." She smiled at him before turning to the small group. "They were grouped together in this book we were reading, and it asked the question, 'How do we know what they wrote is true even though they wrote different accounts?'" Ruth met Joseph's eyes. "So I'm glad Joseph's here because I tried to explain your sports analogy, but I'm not sure I did it right. Can you explain it?"

"You and Isaac already heard it," Joseph said, "and you just explained it to Gabriel."

"Ella hasn't heard it." Ruth motioned to her friend, who did appear curious.

He acknowledged Ella with a smile. "All right. It's like this. Four guys go to watch the same baseball game."

"I thought it was football," Ruth interrupted.

"It works for any sport. I'm trying to mix it up for you."

"Sorry. Go ahead."

Joseph paused for a moment, eyeing Ruth as though he expected another interruption.

"I said I was sorry," she said.

"Four guys go to a baseball game," Joseph said. "The first guy is a fan of team A and so are most of his friends. So when he talks about the game afterwards, he's focused on team A and knows who scored each of their runs but can't remember the names of any players on the other team. But the second guy is a fan of team B. He does know and talk about those other players. The third guy, he's a statistics geek like Isaac." Joseph stopped long enough to accept a punch in the arm from his brother. "His report on the game is filled with who got the most outs and the most hits regardless of which team they were on. Then the fourth guy is a recruiter. He sees potential, not necessarily results. That's what he talks about when he talks about the game. So all four of these guys are saying different things about the same game. It's all true, just from different perspectives. But one detail they all mention, which is arguably the most important fact, is who won the game." He raised his eyebrows at Ella expectantly.

"Jesus?" she said.

"Yeah, it breaks down a little if you try to picture the savior of the world swinging a bat, but you get the idea?"

She nodded.

"That's pretty much how you explained it, only with football." Gabe reached over to squeeze Ruth's hand.

She thanked him for the compliment but still felt that her brother explained it better. When Gabe pulled his hand away, she realized that Joseph and Isaac were both giving him stern stares. That was going to get old so fast.

He picked up the top page of his notebook and put it down again. "We don't know a lot about the authors themselves. We mostly know they had important messages, the gospels, to share. If you were going to write a message to leave for those who come after you, what would you include?"

It was as quiet as if they were still waiting for him to ask a question. Ruth didn't have an answer even after having time to think about it, not that she'd put any effort into reflection. She'd been distracted by other things during the week. Eventually, her eyes drifted to Isaac, who always seemed to have something intelligent to say.

Isaac smiled slowly. He was becoming aware that everyone was waiting for him to start the discussion. "Well... I can't imagine that I'd have anything to say that hasn't already been said by someone else. And better than I could say it."

His admission of having nothing new to say was probably the most intelligent thing he could have said.

"I'm going to give the same answer," Joseph said. "And then we're all going to pretend I said it first."

Into the laughter, Ella said, "Me, too. My message is also listen to those other guys."

"You're all copying me," Gabriel said. "Because I always say newer is not necessarily better."

When they quieted down, Ruth looked at Gabriel as she summed up that no one had anything to say. He tipped his notebook towards her and tapped a blank space. Were they out of questions already? It had seemed as though they had plenty of material on Monday. Enough that they hadn't revisited the questions the two other times they'd seen each other since.

"Oh, dear. Our leadership is falling apart." Isaac feigned distress with a hand against the side of his face.

"We just need a minute," Ruth said. Surely they had another question they simply forgot to write down. She couldn't think of one.

Gabriel showed her that the next page was blank as he shrugged.

"I guess now that you two are all goofy for each other, you can't get any work done," Joseph teased.

"No one is goofy," Ruth said, though somewhere inside was a happy feeling at the idea.

Isaac sighed. "We're going to have to lead by committee from now on."

"What?"

"You turned down a chance to be in charge," Gabriel told him.

Ruth was glad he wasn't completely rolling over to appease her brothers.

"No, committee is a good idea," Isaac said. He pointed at

Gabriel. "You come for lunch at our parents' on Sunday afternoons. Ella, too." He pointed at her, then swung his finger in a circle. "The five of us will be the planning committee. We can keep the lovebirds on task and help them... well, temptation is easier to avoid than to resist."

Ruth chose to ignore the suggestive insinuation in his last line. "If we have only one or two other people on Fridays," she said, "we'll end up having the same discussion twice. How does that sound like a good idea?"

"It makes as much sense as the pre-meetings we have at work with more than half the people who attend the actual meeting."

"Which still makes more sense than the staff meeting for three people we're going to have," Ella said. She sent Ruth a dirty look. "Thank you very much."

Ruth smiled as she defended herself. "I was kidding when I suggested that to your dad."

"I told you not to suggest it."

Gabriel also shared a work meeting story, which reminded Ruth of something the two of them did when they were younger. That reminded Joseph of something he and Isaac used to do. By the time the meeting was wrapping up, Ruth could no longer trace the conversation back to when they'd been on topic. But it didn't seem that anyone minded. They were all still smiling as they put the chairs back.

"Excuse me."

Somehow, no one had noticed the young woman standing in the doorway. The commotion of the tables and chairs halted as everyone turned to her at once.

"Uh, is this where the young adult group meets?" she asked.

"It was," Ruth said. "I mean, it is. We're just finishing up."

"Did I get the time wrong?" She had a large red bag over her shoulder. It slipped to her elbow as she reached into it. One strap fell farther than the other and several pieces of paper and other odds and ends fell to the floor as she pulled out her phone. She seemed oblivious to the items she'd dropped.

Joseph, because he was closest, moved to pick everything up for her.

"We started at seven," Ruth said. Gabriel and Isaac quietly finished cleaning up behind her.

"Seven?" She fiddled with her phone with one hand and pushed her brown hair away from her face with the other.

"I'm Joseph, by the way." He handed her the things he'd picked up.

She took the papers and dropped her phone and a tube of lip balm. Then she squatted to set her bag down while she stuffed everything else into it and kept looking for something on her phone.

The others introduced themselves.

She remained distracted but nodded at each name. "I'm Emily," she said as she stood up again. "And if I come at seven next week…"

When it appeared she had no end for the sentence, Ruth supplied one. "You'd be welcome."

"Is there something I should be reading or doing to prepare?" Emily asked.

"Oh, no." Ruth shook her head. "We'll just have some questions to talk about."

"Most of the time," Isaac said under his breath.

Ruth remembered his talk of leading by committee and wondered how serious the suggestion had been. She was going to worry about it later, if at all. She and Ella walked out with Emily, who was new in town. That gave Ruth a new purpose for their group. While she'd always thought it was a good idea, working things out with Gabriel had given her a selfish investment. Now she could hope they'd be a helpful landing for the newcomer.

Emily waved when they got outside and dashed to her car. She dropped her keys trying to unlock it. Gabriel was waiting near Ruth's car. Ella walked around to get into the passenger side and give Ruth a moment to say goodbye.

"Isaac said he was serious about me joining your family every Sunday," he said. "He's going to have your mom officially invite me, which sounds sketchy." He picked up a lock of hair from Ruth's shoulder and twirled it between his fingers. "But I don't think I can say no to an opportunity to see more of you."

Ruth felt just a little goofy at the sentiment. "You better not," she said.

When he leaned in to kiss her goodbye, she wondered briefly if either of her brothers was still in the parking lot. She didn't care enough to look for them.

He kissed her lightly, then rested his forehead against hers.

Peace and contentment flowed through Ruth. After weeks of doubts and questions, not to mention years of emptiness, it was wonderful to have her old friend back in her life with everything resolved between them.

"I'm going to ask you to marry me soon," he said.

Ruth jerked her head back to see his eyes.

"Maybe not that soon," he said, laughing. "But your reaction was totally worth bringing it up."

She swatted his arm playfully, and he kissed her one more time before he turned to walk home. They did still have some things to talk about. They'd always have more things to talk about. And that was why talk of marriage wouldn't startle her again.